Baby w/Angela
609 N. Kuaoke Pl St., Penthouse
Honolulu, Hawaii, 96817
Phone - 536-2028
Hilary
Bennett
Dec. 17, 1978

Happy Birthday!

THE BOOK OF KING ARTHUR

by HOWARD PYLE

cover by
DON IRWIN

illustrated by
RON KING

classic press, incorporated • san rafael, california

STAFF

Administration
NICK ODDO, Executive Director
BETTE CHYLE · HELEN EPPERSON

Art
AL DAVIDSON, Art Director
MARK NOBLES, Production Director
RITA SMITH · PATRICIA WALSH

DON IRWIN, Cover Illustrations

Production
PETER TOPAZ

Editorial & Composition
SHIRLEY BOLTON, Production Director
DORIS PARKER · PEGGY RICE
ROBERTA TUMBIOLO · BETTY WELLS

Contributing Artists
WAYNE BROWN
BRIGITTE BRYAN
DICK COLE
AL DAVIDSON
DUNBRACCO DEMPSTER
DENNIS A. DIERKS
DON IRWIN
RON KING
MICHAEL RIOS

Contributing Writers
BERNICE HARDING
LOU HARTMAN
FRED McADAMS
DORIS PARKER
MARTHA SHOGREN
ROBERT SHOGREN
CHARLES STRANAHAN

Library of Congress Catalog Card Number: 77-79987

Table of Contents

Foreword

After several years of contemplation and of thought upon the matter herein contained, it has at last come about, by the Grace of God, that I have been able to write this work with such pleasure of spirit that, if it gives to you but a part of the joy that it hath afforded me, I shall be very well content with what I have done.

For when, in pursuing this history, I have come to consider the high nobility of spirit that moved these excellent men to act as they did, I have felt that they have afforded such a perfect example of courage and humility that anyone might do exceedingly well to follow after their manner of behavior in such measure as he is able to do.

For I believe that King Arthur was the most honorable, gentle Knight who ever lived in all the world. And those who were his fellows of the Round Table—taking him as their looking-glass of chivalry—made, altogether, such a company of noble knights that it is hardly to be supposed that their like will ever be seen again in this world. Wherefore it is that I have had such extraordinary pleasure in beholding how those famous knights behaved whenever circumstances called upon them to perform their endeavor.

So in the year of grace one thousand nine hundred and two I began to write this history of King Arthur and his Knights of the Round Table and, if I am able so to do, I shall endeavor, with love of that task, to finish the same at some other time in another book and to the satisfaction of whosoever may care to read the story thereof.

hath afforded: Has given. The word usage in King Arthur seems strange at first. You will get used to it and understand the story more easily if you read the first few pages aloud.

looking-glass of chivalry: The perfect representative of chivalry, the system of knighthood. We use the term "picture perfect" to describe one who sets an excellent example.

7

Prologue

In ancient days there lived a very noble King, named Uther-Pendragon, and he became Overlord of all of Britain. This King was very greatly aided unto the achievement of the Pendragonship of the realm by the help of two men, who rendered him great assistance in all that he did. The one of these men was a certain very powerful enchanter and sometime prophet known to men as Merlin the Wise; and he gave very good counsel unto Uther-Pendragon. The other man was an excellent noble and renowned knight, hight Ulfius (who was thought by many to be the greatest leader in war of any man then alive); and he gave Uther-Pendragon aid and advice in battle. So, with the help of Merlin and Sir Ulfius, Uther-Pendragon was able to overcome all of his enemies and to become King of the entire realm.

After Uther-Pendragon had ruled his kingdom for a number of years he took to wife a certain beautiful and gentle lady, hight Igraine. This noble dame was the widow of Gerlois, the Duke of Tintegal; by which prince she had two daughters—one of whom was named Margaise and the other Morgana le Fay. And Morgana le Fay was a famous sorceress. These daughters the Queen brought with her to the Court of

enchanter: A magician.

hight: Named, called.

9

puissant: Powerful.

ultramarine: Dark violet blue, a royal color.

dolorous: Terrible.
certes: Certainly.

countenance: Here, expression.

harborage: Shelter in a haven.

Uther-Pendragon after she had married that puissant King, and there Margaise was wedded to King Urien of Gore, and Morgana le Fay was wedded to King Lot of Orkney.

Now after awhile Uther-Pendragon and Queen Igraine had a son born unto them, and he was very beautiful and of great size and strength of bone. And whilst the child still lay wrapped in his swaddling clothes and lying in a cradle of gold and ultramarine, Merlin came to Uther-Pendragon with a spirit of prophecy strong upon him (for such was often the case with him), and, speaking in that spirit of prophecy, he said, "Lord, it is given unto me to foresee that thou shalt shortly fall sick of a fever and that thou shalt maybe die of a violent sweat that will follow thereon. Now, should such a dolorous thing befall us all, this young child (who is, certes, the hope of all this realm) will be in very great danger of his life; for many enemies will assuredly rise up with design to seize upon him for the sake of his inheritance, and either he will be slain or else he will be held in captivity from which he shall hardly hope to escape. Wherefore, I do beseech thee, Lord, that thou wilt permit Sir Ulfius and myself to presently convey the child away unto some place of safe refuge, where he may be hidden in secret until he groweth to manhood and is able to guard himself from such dangers as may threaten him."

When Merlin had made an end of speaking thus, Uther-Pendragon made reply with a very steadfast countenance in this wise: "Merlin, so far as my death is concerned—when my time cometh to die I believe God will give me grace to meet my end with entire cheerfulness; for, certes, my lot is in that wise no different from that of any other man who hath been born of woman. But touching the matter of this young child, if thy prophecy be true, then his danger is very great, and it would be well that he should be conveyed hence to some place of safe harborage as thou dost advise. Wherefore, I pray thee to perform thy will in this affair, bearing in thy heart the consideration that the child is the most precious inheritance which I shall leave unto this land."

All this, as was said, Uther-Pendragon spake with great calmness and equanimity of spirit. And Merlin did as he had advised, and he and Sir Ulfius conveyed the child away by night, and no one but they wist whither the babe had been taken. And shortly afterward Uther-Pendragon was seized with the sickness as Merlin had foretold, and he died exactly as Merlin had feared that he would die; wherefore it was very well that the child had been taken to a place of safety.

And after Uther-Pendragon had departed from this life, it was likewise as Merlin had feared, for all the realm fell into great disorder. For each lesser king contended against his fellow for overlordship, and wicked knights and barons harried the highways as they listed and there levied toll with great cruelty upon helpless wayfarers. For some such travellers they took prisoners and held for ransom, whiles others they slew because they had no ransom to pay. So it was a very common sight to see a dead man lying by the roadside, if you should venture to make a journey upon some business or other. Thus it befell that, after awhile, all that dolorous land groaned with the trouble that lay upon it.

Thus there passed nearly eighteen years in such great affliction, and then one day the Archbishop of Canterbury summoned Merlin to him and bespake him in this wise: "Merlin, men say that thou art the wisest man in all the world. Canst thou not find some means to heal the distractions of this woeful realm? Bend thou thy wisdom to this matter and choose thou a king who shall be a fit overlord for us, so that we may enjoy happiness of life once more as we did in the days of Uther-Pendragon."

Then Merlin lifted up his countenance upon the Archbishop, and spake in this wise: "My lord, the spirit of prophecy that lieth upon me sometimes moveth me now to say that I do perceive that this country is soon to have a king who shall be wiser and greater and more worthy of praise

equanimity: Evenness of temper. A good ruler must be able to control his emotions in difficult situations. Uther-Pendragon shows this ability as he speaks of this serious matter.

overlordship: Authority. England at this time was divided into many small kingdoms. An overlord was a king who had authority over certain other kings.

Archbishop of Canterbury: The powerful head of the Church of England.

than was even Uther-Pendragon. And he shall bring order and peace where is now disorder and war. Moreover, I may tell you that this King shall be of Uther-Pendragon's own full blood-royal."

To this the Archbishop said: "What thou tellest me, Merlin, is a wonderfully strange thing. But in this spirit of prophecy canst thou not foretell when this King is to come? And canst thou tell how we shall know him when he appeareth amongst us? For many lesser kings there are who would fain be overlord of this land, and many such there are who deem themselves fit to rule over all the others. How then shall we know the real King from those who may proclaim themselves to be the rightful king?"

"My lord Archbishop," quoth Merlin, "if I have thy leave for to exert my magic I shall set an adventure which, if any man achieve it, all the world shall straightway know that he is the rightful King and overlord of this realm." And to this the Archbishop said, "Merlin, I bid thee do whatsoever may seem to thee to be right in this affair." And Merlin said, "I will do so."

So Merlin caused by magic that a huge marble stone, four square, should suddenly appear in an open place before the cathedral door. And upon this block of marble he caused it to be that there should stand an anvil and into the anvil he caused it that there should be thrust a great naked sword midway deep of the blade. And this sword was the most wonderful that any man had ever seen, for the blade was of blue steel and extraordinarily bright and glistering. And the hilt was of gold, chased and carved with marvellous cunning, and inlaid with a great number of precious stones, so that it shone with wonderful brightness in the sunlight. And about the sword were written these words in letters of gold:—

Whoso Pulleth Out this Sword from the Anvil
That same is Rightwise King—Born of England.

fain: Be pleased to; be eager to.

anvil: An iron block.

glistering: Glistening, glittering.
hilt: Handle, also called haft.
chased: Adorned with embossed or engraved relief work.

So a great many people came and gazed upon that sword and marvelled at it exceedingly, for its like had never before been beheld upon the earth.

Then, when Merlin had accomplished this miracle, he bade the Archbishop to call together all the chief people of that land upon Christmastide; and he bade the Archbishop to command that every man should make assay to draw out the sword, for that he who should succeed in drawing it forth out of the anvil should be rightwise King of Britain.

bade: Asked.
assay: Trial, attempt.

So the Archbishop did according as Merlin said; and this was the marvel of the marble stone and the anvil, of which same anyone may easily read for himself in that book written a very long while ago by Robert de Boron, which is called Le Roman de Merlin.

Now when the mandate of the Lord Archbishop went forth, summoning all the chief people of the land to the assay of that miracle (for, indeed, it was a miracle to draw forth a sword-blade out of an anvil of solid iron), all the realm became immediately cast into a great ferment, so that each man asked his fellow, "Who shall draw forth that sword, and who shall be our King?" Some thought it would be King Lot and others thought it would be King Urien of Gore (these being the sons-in-law unto Uther-Pendragon); some thought that it would be King Leodegrance of Cameliard, and others that it would be King Ryence of North Wales; some thought it would be this king and others that it would be that king; for all the world was divided into different parties who thought according to their liking.

Then, as Christmastide drew nigh, it presently appeared as though the entire world was wending its way to London Town, for the highways and the by-ways became filled with wayfarers—kings and lords and knights and ladies and esquires and pages and men-at-arms—all betaking their way whither the assay was to be made of that adventure of the

nigh: Near.

13

within their compass: Within their walls; inside them.

sword and the anvil. Every inn and castle was filled so full of travellers that it was a marvel how so many folk could be contained within their compass, and everywhere were tents and pavilions pitched along the wayside for the accommodation of those who could not find shelter within doors.

But when the Archbishop beheld the multitudes that were assembling, he said to Merlin, "Indeed, Merlin, it would be a very singular thing if among all these great kings and noble, honorable lords we should not find some one worthy of being the King of this realm."

Unto the which Merlin smiled and said, "Marvel not, my lord, if among all those who appear to be so extraordinarily worthy there shall not be found one who is worthy; and marvel not if, among all those who are unknown, there shall arise one who shall approve himself to be entirely worthy."

And the Archbishop pondered Merlin's words, and so beginneth this story.

Part One

The Winning of Kinghood

*H*ere *beginneth the story of the sword, the anvil, and the marble stone, and of how that sword was first achieved by an unknown youth, until then of no renown, whether in arms or of estate.*

So hearken unto that which I have hereinafter written.

hearken: Listen, heed.

It happened that among those worthies who were summoned unto London Town by the mandate of the Archbishop as above recounted, there was a certain knight, very honorable and of high estate, by name Sir Ector of Bonmaison—surnamed the Trustworthy Knight, because of the fidelity with which he kept the counsel of those who confided in him, and because he always performed unto all men, whether of high or low degree, that which he promised to undertake, without defalcation as to the same. So this noble and excellent knight was held in great regard by all those who knew him; for not only was he thus honorable in conduct but he was, besides, of very high estate, being possessed of seven castles in Wales and in the adjoining country north thereof, and likewise of certain fruitful tracts of land with villages appertaining thereunto, and also of sundry forests of great extent, both in the north country and the west. This very noble knight had two sons; the elder of these was Sir Kay, a young knight of great valor and promise, and already well renowned in the Courts of Chivalry because of several very honorable deeds of worthy achievement in arms which he had performed; the other was a young lad of eighteen years of age, by name Arthur, who at that time was serving with good repute as Sir Kay's esquire-at-arms.

1

HOW SIR KAY DID COMBAT IN A GREAT TOURNAMENT AT LONDON TOWN AND OF HOW HE BRAKE HIS SWORD. LIKEWISE, HOW ARTHUR FOUND A NEW SWORD FOR HIM.

defalcation: Betraying a trust by breaking a promise.

gryphon: A fabulous creature, half eagle and half lion; also spelled griffin or griffon.

pavilion: A large tent often used by traveling nobles of the day since inns were not plentiful.

Now when Sir Ector of Bonmaison received by messenger the mandate of the Archbishop, he immediately summoned these two sons unto him and bade them to prepare straightway for to go with him to London Town, and they did so. And in the same manner he bade a great number of retainers and esquires and pages for to make them ready, and they likewise did so. Thus, with a very considerable array at arms and with great show of circumstance, Sir Ector of Bonmaison betook his way unto London Town in obedience to the commands of the Archbishop.

So, when he had come thither he took up his inn in a certain field where many other noble knights and puissant lords had already established themselves, and there he set up a very fair pavilion of green silk, and erected his banner emblazoned with the device of his house; to wit, a gryphon, black, upon a field of green.

And upon this field were a great multitude of other pavilions of many different colors, and over above each pavilion was the pennant and the banner of that puissant lord to whom the pavilion belonged. Wherefore, because of the multitude of these pennants and banners the sky was at places well-nigh hidden with the gaudy colors of the fluttering flags.

Among the great lords who had come thither in pursuance to the Archbishop's summons were many very famous kings and queens and noblemen of high degree. For there was King Lot of Orkney, who had taken to wife a step-daughter of Uther-Pendragon, and there was King Uriens of Gore, who had taken to wife another step-daughter of that great king, and there was King Ban, and King Bors, and King Ryance, and King Leodegrance and many others of like degree, for there were no less than twelve kings and seven dukes, so that, what with their court of lords and ladies and esquires and pages in attendance, the town of London had hardly ever seen the like before that day.

Now the Archbishop of Canterbury, having in mind the extraordinary state of the occasion that had brought so many kings and dukes and high lords unto that adventure of the sword and the anvil, had commanded that there should be a very stately and noble tournament proclaimed. Likewise he commanded that this contest at arms should be held in a certain field nigh to the great cathedral, three days before that assay should be made of the sword and the anvil (which same was to be undertaken, as aforesaid, upon Christmas day). To this tournament were bidden all knights who were of sufficient birth, condition, and quality for to fit them to take part therein. Accordingly, very many exalted knights made application for admission, and that in such numbers that three heralds were kept busy looking into their pretensions unto the right of battle. For these heralds examined the escutcheons and the rolls of lineage of all applicants with great care and circumspection.

Now when Sir Kay received news of this tournament he went to where his father was, and when he stood before his face he spake in this wise: "Sire, being thy son and of such very high condition both as to birth and estate as I have inherited from thee, I find that I have an extraordinary desire to imperil my body in this tourney. Accordingly, if so be I may approve my quality as to knighthood before this college of heralds, it will maybe be to thy great honor and credit, and to the honor and credit of our house if I should undertake this adventure. Wherefore I do crave thy leave to do as I have a mind."

Unto these Sir Ector made reply: "My son, thou hast my leave for to enter this honorable contest, and I do hope that God will give thee a great deal of strength, and likewise such grace of spirit that thou mayst achieve honor to thyself and credit to us who are of thy blood."

So Sir Kay departed with very great joy and immediately went to that congress of heralds and submitted his

THE WINNING OF KINGHOOD

sufficient birth: Noble ancestry or parentage.

heralds: Here, officials with a special knowledge of heraldry involving, in part, tracing family lines of the nobility.

circumspection: Thoroughness.

pretensions unto them. And, after they had duly examined into his claims to knighthood, they entered his name as a knight-contestant according to his desire; and at this Sir Kay was filled with great content and joy of heart.

So, when his name had been enrolled upon the list of combatants, Sir Kay chose his young brother Arthur for to be his esquire-at-arms and to carry his spear and pennant before him into the field of battle, and Arthur was also made exceedingly glad because of the honor that had befallen him and his brother.

Now, the day having arrived when this tourney was to be held, a very huge concourse of people gathered together to witness that noble and courtly assault at arms. For at that time London was, as aforesaid, extraordinarily full of nobility and knighthood, wherefore it was reckoned that not less than twenty thousand lords and ladies (besides those twelve kings and their courts and seven dukes and their courts) were assembled in the lists circumadjacent to the field of battle for to witness the performance of those chosen knights. And those noble people sat so close together, and so filled the seats and benches assigned to them, that it appeared as though an entirely solid wall of human souls surrounded that meadow where the battle was to be fought. And, indeed, any knight might well be moved to do his uttermost upon such a great occasion with the eyes of so many beautiful dames and noble lords gazing upon his performances. Wherefore the hearts of all the knights attendant were greatly expanded with emulation to overturn their enemies into the dust.

In the centre of this wonderful court of lords and ladies there was erected the stall and the throne of the lord Archbishop himself. Above the throne was a canopy of purple cloth emblazoned with silver lilies, and the throne itself was hung all about with purple cloth of velvet, embroidered, alternately, with the figure of St. George in gold, and with silver crosses of St. George surrounded by golden halos. Here the lord Archbishop himself sat in great estate and pomp, being surrounded by a very exalted court of clerks of high degree and also of knights of honorable estate, so that all that centre of the field glistered with the splendor of gold and silver embroidery, and was made beautiful by various colors of rich apparel and bright with fine armor of excellent workmanship. And, indeed, such was the stateliness of all these circumstances that very few who were there had ever seen so noble a preparation for battle as that which they then beheld.

Now, when all that great assembly were in their places and everything had been prepared in due wise, an herald came and stood forth before the enstalled throne of the Archbishop and blew a very strong, loud blast upon a trumpet. At that signal the turnpikes of the lists were immediately opened and two parties of knights-contestant entered therein—the one party at the northern extremity of the meadow of battle and the other party at the southern extremity thereof. Then immediately all that lone field was a-glitter with the bright-shining splendor of the sunlight upon polished armor and accoutrements. So these two parties took up their station, each at such a place as had been assigned unto them—the one to the north and the other to the south.

Now the party with which Sir Kay had cast his lot was at the north of the field, and that company was fourscore and thirteen in number; and the other party stood at the south end of the field, and that company was fourscore and sixteen in number. But though the party with whom Sir Kay had attached himself numbered less by three than the other party, yet was it the stronger by some degree because that there were a number of knights of great strength and renown in that company. Indeed it may be here mentioned that two of those knights afterward became companions in very good credit of the round table—to wit: Sir Mador de la Porte, and Sir Bedevere—which latter was the last who saw King Arthur alive upon this earth.

Trumpets

1. A modern military trumpet.
2. 15th century military trumpet.

accoutrements: Equipment.

ordination: Orders, rules.

So, when all was prepared according to the ordination of the tournament, and when those knights-contestant had made themselves ready in all ways that were necessary, and when they had dressed their spears and their shields in such a manner as befitted knights about to enter serious battle, the herald set his trumpet to his lips a second time and blew upon it with might and main. Then, having sounded this blast, he waited for a while and then he blew upon the trumpet again.

And, upon that blast, each of those parties of knights quitted its station and rushed forth in great tumult against the other party, and that with such noise and fury that the whole earth groaned beneath the feet of the war-horses, and trembled and shook as with an earthquake.

So those two companies met, the one against the other, in the midst of the field, and the roar of breaking lances was so terrible that those who heard it were astonished and appalled at the sound. For several fair dames swooned away with terror of the noise, and others shrieked aloud; for not only was there that great uproar, but the air was altogether filled with the splinters of ash wood that flew about.

swooned away: Fainted.

threescore and ten: Seventy. A score is twenty.

cantels: Pieces.

In that famous assault threescore and ten very noble and honorable knights were overthrown, many of them being trampled beneath the hoofs of the horses; wherefore, when the two companies withdrew in retreat each to his station the ground was beheld to be covered all over with broken fragments of lances and with cantels of armor, and many knights were seen to be wofully lying in the midst of all that wreck. And some of these champions strove to arise and could not, while others lay altogether quiet as though in death. To these ran divers esquires and pages in great numbers, and lifted up the fallen men and bare them away to places of safe harborage. And likewise attendants ran and gathered up the cantels of armor and the broken spears, and bare them away to the barriers, so that, by and by, the field was altogether cleared once more.

Then all those who gazed down upon that meadow gave loud acclaim with great joyousness of heart, for such a noble and glorious contest at arms in friendly assay had hardly ever been beheld in all that realm before.

Now turn we unto Sir Kay; for in this assault he had conducted himself with such credit that no knight who was there had done better than he, and maybe no one had done so well as he. For, though two opponents at once had directed their spears against him, yet he had successfully resisted their assault. And one of those two he smote so violently in the midst of his defences that he had lifted that assailant entirely over the crupper of the horse which he rode, and had flung him down to the distance of half a spear's length behind his steed, so that the fallen knight had rolled thrice over in the dust ere he ceased to fall.

crupper: Rump.

23

errant: Wandering in search of the adventure of redressing wrongs or enforcing rights.

And when those of Sir Kay's party who were nigh to him beheld what he did, they gave him loud and vehement acclaim, and that in such measure that Sir Kay was wonderfully well satisfied and pleased at heart.

And, indeed, it is to be said that at that time there was hardly any knight in all the world who was so excellent in deeds of arms as Sir Kay. And though there afterward came knights of much greater renown and of more glorious achievement (as shall be hereinafter recorded in good season), yet at that time Sir Kay was reckoned by many to be one of the most wonderfully puissant knights (whether errant or in battle) in all of that realm.

So was that course of the combat run to the great pleasure and satisfaction of all who beheld it, and more especially of Sir Kay and his friends. And after it had been completed the two parties in array returned each to its assigned station once more.

delivered up: Gave.

And when they had come there, each knight delivered up his spear unto his esquire. For the assault which was next to be made was to be undertaken with swords, wherefore all lances and other weapons were to be put away; such being the order of that courteous and gentle bout at arms.

Accordingly, when the herald again blew upon his trumpet, each knight drew his weapon with such readiness for battle that there was a great splendor of blades all flashing in the air at once. And when the herald blew a second time each party pushed forward to the contest with great nobleness of heart and eagerness of spirit, every knight being moved with intent to engage his oppugnant with all the might and main that lay in him.

oppugnant: Opponent.

Then immediately began so fierce a battle that if those knights had been very enemies of long standing instead of friendly contestants, the blows which they delivered the one upon the other could not have been more vehement as to strength or more astonishing to gaze upon.

And in this affair likewise Sir Kay approved himself to be so extraordinary a champion that his like was nowhere to be seen in all that field; for he violently smote down five knights, the one after the other, ere he was stayed in his advance.

Wherefore, beholding him to be doing work of such a sort, several of the knights of the other party endeavored to come at him with intent to meet him in his advance.

Amongst these was a certain knight, hight Sir Balamorgineas, who was so huge of frame that he rode head and shoulders above any other knight. And he was possessed of such extraordinary strength that it was believed that he could successfully withstand the assault of three ordinary knights at one time. Wherefore when this knight beheld the work that Sir Kay did, he cried out to him, "Ho! ho! Sir Knight of the black gryphon, turn thou hitherward and do a battle with me!"

hitherward: This way.

Now when Sir Kay beheld Sir Balamorgineas to be minded to come against him in that wise—very threateningly and minded to do him battle—he turned him toward his enemy with great cheerfulness of spirit. For at that time Sir Kay was very full of youthful fire and reckoned nothing of assaulting any enemy who might demand battle of him.

(So it was at that time. But it after befell, when he became Seneschal, and when other and mightier knights appeared at the court of the King, that he would sometimes avoid an encounter with such a knight as Sir Launcelot, or Sir Pellias, or Sir Marhaus, or Sir Gawaine, if he might do so with credit to his honor.)

Seneschal: The king's representative in the administration of justice and his most powerful and important servant.

So, being very full of the spirit of youth, he turned him with great lustiness of heart, altogether inflamed with the eagerness and fury of battle. And he cried out in a great voice, "Very well, I will do battle with thee, and I will cast thee down like thy fellows!" And therewith he smote with wonderful fierceness at Sir Balamorgineas, and that with all

haft: The handle of a sword.

turrets: Small towers.

umbril: The helmet visor that covers the face; sometimes called the beaver.

his might. And Sir Balamorgineas received the stroke upon his helmet and was altogether bewildered by the fury thereof, for he had never felt its like before that time. Wherefore his brains swam so light that it was necessary for him to hold to the horn of his saddle to save himself from falling.

But it was a great pity for Sir Kay that, with the fierceness of the blow, his sword-blade snapped short at the haft, flying so high in the air that it appeared to overtop the turrets of the cathedral in its flight. Yet so it happened, and thus it befell that Sir Kay was left without any weapon. Yet it was thought that, because of that stroke, he had Sir Balamorgineas entirely at his mercy, and that if he could have struck another blow with his sword he might easily have overcome him.

But as it was, Sir Balamorgineas presently so far recovered himself that he perceived his enemy to be altogether at his mercy; wherefore, being filled beyond measure with rage because of the blow he had received, he pushed against Sir Kay with intent to smite him down in a violent assault.

In this pass it would maybe have gone very ill with Sir Kay but that three of his companions in arms, perceiving the extreme peril in which he lay, thrust in betwixt him and Sir Balamorgineas with intent to take upon themselves the assault of that knight and so to save Sir Kay from overthrow. This they did with such success that Sir Kay was able to push out from the press and to escape to the barriers without suffering any further harm at the hands of his enemies.

Now when he reached the barrier, his esquire, young Arthur, came running to him with a goblet of spiced wine. And Sir Kay opened the umbril of his helmet for to drink, for he was athirst beyond measure. And, lo! his face was all covered over with blood and sweat, and he was so a-drought with battle that his tongue clave to the roof of his mouth and he could not speak. But when he had drunk of the draught that Arthur gave him, his tongue was loosened and he cried

26

out to the young man in a loud and violent voice: "Ho! ho! Brother, get me another sword for to do battle, for I am assuredly winning for our house much glory this day!" And Arthur said, "Where shall I get thee a sword?" And Kay said, "Make haste unto our father's pavilion and fetch me thence another sword, for this which I have is broken." And Arthur said, "I will do so with all speed," and thereupon he set hand to the barrier and leaped over it into the alleyway beyond. And he ran down the alleyway with all the speed that he was able with intent to fulfil that task which his brother had bidden him to undertake; and with like speed he ran to that pavilion that his father had set up in the meadows.

But when he came to the pavilion of Sir Ector he found no one there, for all the attendants had betaken themselves unto the tournament. And neither could he find any sword fit for his brother's handling, wherefore he was put to a great pass to know what to do in that matter.

In this extremity he bethought him of that sword that stood thrust into the anvil before the cathedral, and it appeared to him that such a sword as that would suit his brother's purposes very well. Wherefore he said to himself, "I will go thither and get that sword if I am able to do so, for it will assuredly do very well for my brother for to finish his battle withal." Whereupon he ran with all speed to the cathedral. And when he had come there he discovered that no one was there upon guard at the block of marble, as had heretofore been the case, for all who had been upon guard had betaken themselves unto the contest of arms that was toward. And the anvil and the sword stood where he could reach them. So, there being no one to stay young Arthur, he leaped up upon the block of marble and laid his hands unto the hilt of the sword. And he bent his body and drew upon the sword very strongly, and, lo! it came forth from the anvil with wonderful smoothness and ease, and he held the sword in his hand, and it was his.

bethought: Remembered.

And when he had got the sword in that way, he wrapped it in his cloak so that no one might see it (for it shone with an exceeding brightness and splendor) and he leaped down from the block of marble stone and hastened with it unto the field of battle.

Now when Arthur had entered into that meadow once more, he found Sir Kay awaiting his coming with great impatience of spirit. And when Sir Kay saw him he cried out, very vehemently, "Hast thou got a sword?" And Arthur said, "Yea, I have one here." Thereupon he opened his cloak and showed Sir Kay what sword it was he had brought.

Now when Sir Kay beheld the sword he immediately knew it, and he wist not what to think or what to say, wherefore he stood for a while, like one turned into a stone, looking upon that sword. Then in awhile he said, in a very strange voice, "Where got ye that sword?" And Arthur looked upon his brother and he beheld that his countenance was greatly disturbed, and that his face was altogether as white as wax. And he said, "Brother, what ails thee that thou lookest so strangely. I will tell the entire truth. I could find no sword in our father's pavilion, wherefore I bethought me of that sword that stood in the anvil upon the marble cube before the cathedral. So I went thither and made assay for to draw it forth, and it came forth with wonderful ease. So, when I had drawn it out, I wrapped it in my cloak and brought it hither unto thee as thou beholdest."

Then Sir Kay turned his thoughts inward and communed with himself in this wise, "Lo! my brother Arthur is as yet hardly more than a child. And he is, moreover, exceedingly innocent. Therefore he knoweth not what he hath done in this nor what the doing thereof signifieth. Now, since he hath achieved this weapon, why should I not myself lay claim to that achievement, and so obtain the glory which it signifieth." Whereupon he presently aroused himself, and he said to Arthur, "Give the sword and the cloak to me," and

wist: Knew.

28

Arthur did as his brother commanded. And when he had done so Sir Kay said to him, "Tell no man of this but keep it privy in thine own heart. Meantime go thou to our father where he sits at the lists and bid come straightway unto the pavilion where we have taken up our inn."

And Arthur did as Sir Kay commanded him, greatly possessed with wonder that his brother should be so disturbed in spirit as he had appeared to be. For he wist not what he had done in drawing out that sword from the anvil, nor did he know of what great things should arise from that little thing, for so it is in this world that a man sometimes approves himself to be worthy of such a great trust as that, and yet, in lowliness of spirit, he is yet altogether unaware that he is worthy thereof. And so it was with young Arthur at that time.

lists: Enclosed tournament fields.

So Arthur made haste to that part of the lists where Sir Ector sat with the people of his household. And he stood before his father and said, "Sire, my brother Kay hath sent me hitherward for to bid thee come straightway unto the pavilion where we have taken up our inn. And, truly, I think something very extraordinary hath befallen, for my brother Kay hath such a countenance as I never saw him wear."

Then Sir Ector marvelled very greatly what it was that should cause Sir Kay to quit that battle and to summon him at such a time, wherefore he arose from where he sat and went with Arthur. And they went to the pavilion, and when he had come there, behold! Sir Kay was standing in the midst of the pavilion. And Sir Ector saw that his face was as white as ashes of wood and that his eyes shone with a wonderful brightness. And Sir Ector said, "My son, what ails thee?" whereunto Sir Kay made reply, "Sire, here is a very wonderful matter." Therewith he took his father by the hand and brought him to the table that stood in the pavilion. And upon the table there lay a cloak and there was something within the cloak. Then Sir Kay opened the cloak and, lo! there lay the sword of the anvil, and the hilt thereof and the blade thereof glistered with exceeding splendor.

2

HOW ARTHUR TWICE PER-
FORMED THE MIRACLE OF
THE SWORD BEFORE SIR
ECTOR AND OF HOW HIS
BIRTHRIGHT WAS DIS-
COVERED UNTO HIM.

31

foretend: Foreshadow; lead to in the future.

And Sir Ector immediately knew that sword and whence it came. Wherefore he was filled with such astonishment that he wist not what to do. And for a while his tongue refused to speak, and after a while he found speech and cried out aloud in a great voice, "What is this that mine eyes behold!"

To this Sir Kay made reply, "Sire. I have that sword which stood a while since embedded in the anvil that stands upon the cube of marble stone before the great cathedral. Wherefore I demand that thou tellest me what this may foretend?"

Then Sir Ector said, "How came you by that sword?"

And for a while Sir Kay was silent, but after a while he said, "Sire, I brake my sword in that battle which of late I fought, whereupon I found me this sword in its stead."

Then Sir Ector was altogether bemazed and knew not whether to believe what his ears heard. And after awhile he said, "If so be that thou didst draw forth this sword from the anvil, then it must also be that thou art rightwise King of Britain, for so the saying of the sword proclaimeth. But if thou didst indeed draw it forth from the anvil, then it will be that thou shalt as easily be able for to thrust it back again into that place from whence thou didst take it."

At this a great trouble of spirit fell upon Sir Kay, and he cried out in a very loud voice, "Who may do such a thing as that, and who could perform so great a miracle as to thrust a sword into solid iron?" Whereunto Sir Ector made reply, "Such a miracle is no greater than the miracle that thou hast performed in drawing it out from its embedment. For who ever heard that a man could draw forth a sword from a place and yet would not thrust it back whence he drew it?"

Then Sir Kay wist not what to say to his father, and he greatly feared that he should not be able to perform that miracle. But, nevertheless, he took what comfort to himself he was able, saying, "If my young brother Arthur was able to perform this miracle why should I not do a miracle of a like sort, for, assuredly, I am not less worthy than he. Wherefore if he drew the sword forth with such ease, it may be that I with equal ease shall be able to thrust it back into its place again." Accordingly he took such comfort to himself in these thoughts as he was able.

So he wrapped the sword in the cloak again, and when he had done so he and Sir Ector went forth from the pavilion and betook their way unto where was the marble stone and the anvil before the cathedral. And Arthur went with his father and his brother and they forbade him not. And when they had come to that place where the sword had been, Sir Kay mounted upon the cube of marble stone and beheld the face of the anvil. And lo! the face of the anvil was altogether smooth and without a scratch or scar of any sort. And Sir Kay said to himself, "What is this my father would have me do! What man is there in life who could thrust a sword-blade into a solid anvil of iron?" But, ne'theless, he could not withdraw from that impossible undertaking, but was constrained to assay that miracle, wherefore he set the point of the sword to the iron and bore upon it with all his strength. But it was impossible for him to accomplish that thing, and though he endeavored with all his might with the sword against the face of the anvil, yet did he not pierce the iron even to the breadth of a hair.

So, after he had thus assayed for a great while, he at last ceased what he did and came down from where he stood. And he said to his father, "Sire, no man in life may perform that miracle."

Unto this Sir Ector made reply, "How is it possible then that thou couldst have drawn out that sword as thou sayst and yet cannot put it back again?"

Then young Arthur lifted up his voice and said, "My father, have I thy leave to speak?" And Sir Ector said, "Speak, my son." And Arthur said, "I would that I might assay to handle that sword?" Whereunto Sir Ector replied,

"By what authority wouldst thou handle that sword?" And Arthur said, "Because it was I who drew that sword forth from the anvil for my brother. Wherefore, as thou sayest, to draw it forth is not more difficult than to thrust it back again. So I believe that I shall be able to set it back into the iron whence I drew it."

Then Sir Ector gazed upon young Arthur in such a strange manner that Arthur wist not why he looked at him in that wise. Wherefore he cried out, "Sire, why dost thou gaze so strangely upon me? Hast thou anger against me?" Whereunto Sir Ector made reply, "In the sight of God, my son, I have no anger against thee." Then he said, "If thou hast a desire to handle the sword, thou mayst assuredly make assay of that miracle."

So Arthur took the sword from his brother Kay and he leaped up upon the marble stone. And he set the point of the sword upon the anvil and bare very strongly upon it and lo! the sword penetrated very smoothly into the centre of the anvil until it stood midway deep therein, and there it stood fast. And after he had performed that miracle he drew the sword forth again very swiftly and easily, and then thrust it back again once more as he had done before.

But when Sir Ector beheld what Arthur did, he cried out in a voice of exceeding loudness, "Lord! Lord! what is the miracle mine eyes behold!" And when Arthur came down from the cube of marble stone, Sir Ector kneeled down before him and set his hands together, palm to palm.

But when Arthur beheld what his father did, he cried out aloud like one in a great measure of pain; and he said, "My father! my father! why dost thou kneel down to me?"

made manifest: Shown clearly.

To him Sir Ector made reply, "I am not thy father, and now it is made manifest that thou art assuredly of very exalted race and that the blood of kings flows in thy veins, else thou couldst not have handled that sword as thou hast done."

Then Arthur fell a-weeping beyond all measure and he cried out as with great agony of spirit, "Father! father! what is this thou sayst? I beseech thee to arise and not to kneel unto me."

So Sir Ector arose from his knees and stood before the face of Arthur, and he said, "Arthur, why dost thou weep?" And Arthur said, "Because I am afeard."

Now all this while Sir Kay had stood near by and he could neither move nor speak, but stood like one entranced, and he said to himself, "What is this? Is my brother a King?"

wise: Here, way or manner.

signet ring: A ring with a small seal for formal or official use.

mantle: A cloak or cape.

Then Sir Ector spake, saying, "Arthur, the time hath come for thee to know thyself, for the true circumstances of thy life have, heretofore, been altogether hidden from thee.

"Now I do confess everything to thee in this wise: that eighteen year ago there came to me a certain man very wise and high in favor with Uther-Pendragon and that man was the Enchanter Merlin. And Merlin showed me the signet ring of Uther-Pendragon and he commanded me by virtue of that ring that I should be at a certain assigned place at a particular time which he nominated; and the place which he assigned was the postern gate of Uther-Pendragon's castle; and the time which he named was midnight of that very day.

"And he bade me tell no man aught concerning those things which he communicated to me, and so I kept his counsel as he desired me to do.

"So I went to that postern gate at midnight as Merlin had commanded, and at that place there came unto me Merlin and another man, and the other man was Sir Ulfius, who was the chief knight of Uther-Pendragon's household. And I tell thee that these two worthies stood nigher unto Uther-Pendragon than any other men in all of the world.

"Now when those two came unto me, I perceived that Merlin bare in his arms a certain thing wrapped in a scarlet mantle of fine texture. And he opened the folds of the mantle and, lo! I beheld a child not long born and wrapped in swaddling clothes. And I saw the child in the light of a lanthorn which Sir Ulfius bare, and I perceived that he was very fair of face and large of bone—and thou wert that child.

"Then Merlin commanded me in this wise: that I was to take that child and that I should rear him as mine own; and he said that the child was to be called by the name of Arthur; and he said that no one in all the world was to know otherwise than that the child was mine own. And I told Merlin that I would do as he would have me, whereupon I took the child and bare it away with me. And I proclaimed that the child was mine own, and all over the world believed my words, wherefore no one ever knew otherwise than that thou wert mine own son. And that lady who was my wife, when she died she took that secret with her unto Paradise, and since then until now no one in all the world knew aught of this matter but I and those two aforementioned worthies.

"Nor have I until now ever known aught of who was thy father; but now I do suspect who he was and that thou hast in thy veins very high and kingly blood. And I do have in mind that perhaps thy father was Uther-Pendragon himself. For who but the son of Uther-Pendragon could have drawn forth that sword from out of the anvil as thou hast done?"

Then, when Arthur heard that saying of his father's, he cried out in a very loud and vehement voice, "Woe! Woe! Woe!"—saying that word three times. And Sir Ector said, "Arthur, why art thou woful?" And Arthur said, "Because I have lost my father, for I would rather have my father than be a King!"

Now as these things passed, there came unto that place two men, very tall and of a wonderfully noble and haughty appearance. And when these two men had come nigh to where they were, Arthur and Sir Ector and Sir Kay perceived that one of them was the Enchanter Merlin and that the other was Sir Ulfius—for those two men were very famous and well known unto all the world. And when those two had come to where were the three, Merlin spake, saying, "What cheer?" And Sir Ector made answer, "Here is cheer of a very wonderful sort; for, behold, Merlin! this is that child that thou didst bring unto me eighteen years ago, and, lo! thou seest he hath grown unto manhood."

Then Merlin said, "Sir Ector, I know very well who is this youth, for I have kept diligent watch over him for all this time. And I know that in him lieth the hope of Britain. Moreover, I tell thee that even to-day within the surface of an enchanted looking-glass I have beheld all that he hath done

vehement: Fervent, impassioned.

since the morning; and I know how he drew forth the sword from the anvil, and how he thrust it back again; and I know how he drew it forth and thrust it back a second time. And I know all that thou hast been saying unto him this while; wherefore I also do now avouch that thou hast told him the very truth. And, lo! the spirit of prophecy is upon me and I do foresee into the future that thou, Arthur, shall become the greatest and most famous King that ever lived in Britain; and I do foresee that many knights of extraordinary excellence shall gather about thee and that men shall tell of their marvellous deeds as long as this land shall continue, and I do foresee that through these knights thy reign shall be full of splendor and glory; and I do foresee that the most marvellous adventure of the Holy Grail shall be achieved by three of the knights of thy Court, and that to thy lasting renown, who shall be the King under whose reign the holy cup shall be achieved. All these things I foresee; and, lo! the time is now at hand when the glory of thy House shall again be made manifest unto the world, and all the people of this land shall rejoice in thee and thy kinghood. Wherefore, Sir Ector, for these three days to come, I do charge it upon thee that thou do guard this young man as the apple of thine eye, for in him doth lie the hope and salvation of all this realm."

Then Sir Ector lifted up his voice and cried unto Arthur, "A boon! a boon!" And Arthur said, "Alas! how is this? Dost thou, my father, ask a boon of me who may have all in the world that is mine to give? Ask what thou wilt and it is thine!" Then Sir Ector said, "I do beseech this of thee: that when thou art King thy brother Kay may be Seneschal of all this realm." And Arthur said, "It shall be as thou dost ask." And he said, "As for thee, it shall be still better with thee, for thou shalt be my father unto the end!" Whereupon so saying, he took Sir Ector's head into his hands and he kissed Sir Ector upon the forehead and upon the cheeks, and so sealed his plighted word.

boon: A favor. Notice that Sir Ector wants to assure the future position of his natural son, Sir Kay, by making this request.

But all this while Sir Kay had stood like unto one struck by thunder, and he wist not whether to be uplifted unto the skies or to be cast down into the depths, that his young brother should thus have been passed by him and exalted unto that extraordinary altitude of fortune. Wherefore he stood like to one bereft of life and motion.

And let it here be said that Arthur fulfilled all that he had thus promised to his father—for, in after times, he made Sir Kay his Seneschal, and Sir Ector was to him a father until the day of his death, which same befell five years from that time.

Thus I have told you how the royalty of Arthur was first discovered. And now, if you will listen, ye shall hear how it was confirmed before all the world.

bereft: Without or deprived of.

So when the morning of Christmas day had come, many thousands of folk of all qualities, both gentle and simple, gathered together in front of the cathedral for to behold the assay of that sword.

Now there had been a canopy of embroidered cloth of divers colors spread above the sword and the anvil, and a platform had been built around about the cube of marble stone. And nigh unto that place there had been a throne for the Archbishop established; for the Archbishop was to overlook that assay and to see that every circumstance was fulfilled with due equity and circumspection.

So, when the morning was half gone by, the Archbishop himself came with great pomp of estate and took his seat upon the high throne that had been placed for him, and all his court of clerks and knights gathered about him, so that he presented a very proud and excellent appearance of courtliness.

Now unto that assay there had gathered nineteen kings and sixteen dukes, and each of these was of such noble and exalted estate that he entertained high hopes that he would that day be approved before the world to be the right king

3

HOW SEVERAL KINGS AND HIGH DUKES ASSAYED TO DRAW THE SWORD OUT OF THE ANVIL AND HOW THEY FAILED. LIKEWISE HOW ARTHUR MADE THE ASSAY AND SUCCEEDED THEREIN.

equity: Fairness, impartiality.

great pomp of estate: A splendid display befitting one's station.

exalted: Elevated, highly placed.

and overlord of all Britain. Wherefore after the Archbishop had established himself upon his throne, there came several of these and made demand that he should straightway put that matter to the test. So the Archbishop commanded his herald for to sound a trumpet, and to bid all who had the right to make assay of the sword to come unto that adventure, and the herald did according as the Archbishop ordered.

And when the herald had sounded his trumpet there immediately appeared the first of those kings to make trial of the sword, and he who came was King Lot of Orkney and the Isles. With King Lot there came eleven knights and five esquires, so that he appeared in very noble estate before the eyes of all. And when King Lot had arrived at that place, he mounted the platform. And first he saluted the Archbishop, and then he laid his hands to the pommel of the sword in the sight of all. And he bent his body and drew upon the sword with great strength, but he could not move the blade in the anvil even so much as the breadth of a hair, for it stood as fast as the iron in which it was planted. And after that first assay he tried three times more, but still he was altogether unable to move the blade in the iron. Then, after that he had thus four times made assay, he ceased his endeavor and came down from that place. And he was filled with great anger and indignation that he had not succeeded in his endeavor.

And after King Lot there came his brother-in-law, King Urien of Gore, and he also made assay in the same wise as King Lot had done. But neither did he succeed any better than that other king. And after King Urien there came King Fion of Scotland, and after King Fion there came King Mark of Cornwall, and after King Mark there came King Ryence of North Wales, and after King Ryence there came King Leodegrance of Cameliard, and after him came all those other kings and dukes before numerated, and not one of all these was able to move the blade. And some of these high and

pommel: The knob at the end of a sword handle.

numerated: Numbered.

42

mighty lords were filled with anger and indignation that they had not succeeded, and others were ashamed that they had failed in that undertaking before the eyes of all those who looked upon them. But whether they were angry or whether they were ashamed it in no wise helped their case.

Now when all the kings and dukes had thus failed in that adventure, the people who were there were very much astonished, and they said to one another, "How is this? If all those kings and dukes of very exalted estate have failed to achieve that adventure, who then may hope to succeed? For here have been all those who were most worthy of that high honor, and all have tried to draw that sword and all have failed. Who then is there now to come after these who may hope to succeed?"

And, likewise, those kings and dukes spoke together in the same manner. And by and by there came six of the most worthy—to wit, King Lot, King Urien, King Pellinore, King Ban, King Ryence, and Duke Clarence of Northumberland— and these stood before the throne of the Archbishop and spake to him in this wise: "Sir, here have all the kings and dukes of this realm striven before you for to draw forth that sword, and lo! not one of all those who have undertaken that thing hath succeeded in his undertaking. What, then, may we understand but that the enchanter Merlin hath set this adventure for to bring shame and discredit upon all of us who are here, and upon you, who are the head of the church in this realm? For who in all the world may hope to draw forth a sword-blade out from a bed of solid iron? Behold! it is beyond the power of any man. Is it not then plain to be seen that Merlin hath made a mock of us all? Now, therefore, lest all this great congregation should have been called here in vain, we do beseech you of your wisdom that you presently choose the one from among the kings here gathered, who may be best fitted to be overlord of this realm. And when ye shall have chosen him, we will promise to obey him in all

congregation: Throng.

ordain: Decree, order.

things whatsoever he may ordain. Verily, such a choice as that will be better worth while than to spend time in this foolish task of striving to draw forth a sword out of an anvil which no man in all the world may draw forth."

Then was the Archbishop much troubled in spirit, for he said to himself, "Can it be sooth that Merlin hath deceived me, and hath made a mock of me and of all these kings and lordly folk? Surely this cannot be. For Merlin is passing wise, and he would not make a mock of all the realm for the sake of so sorry a jest as this would be. Certes he hath some intent in this of which we know naught, being of less wisdom than he—wherefore I will be patient for a while longer." Accordingly, having communed thus within himself, he spake aloud in this wise to those seven high lords: "Messires," he said, "I have yet faith that Merlin hath not deceived us, wherefore I pray your patience for one little while longer. For if, in the time a man may count five hundred twice over, no one cometh forward to perform this task, then will I, at your behest, proceed to choose one from amongst you and will proclaim him King and Overlord of all." For the Archbishop had faith that Merlin was about to immediately declare a king before them all.

passing: Exceedingly, surpassingly.

Now leave we these and turn we unto Arthur and his father and brother.

For Merlin had bidden those three to abide in their pavilion until such time as he thought would be fit for them to come out thence. And that time being now come, Merlin and Sir Ulfius went to the pavilion of Sir Ector, and Merlin said, "Arthur, arise and come forth, for now the hour is come for thee to assay before the whole world that miracle which thou didst of late execute in privacy." So Arthur did as Merlin bade him to do, and he came forth from the pavilion with his father and his brother, and, lo! he was like one who walked in a dream.

So they five went down from thence toward the cathedral and unto that place of assay. And when they had come to the congregation there assembled, the people made way for them, greatly marvelling and saying to one another, "Who are these with the Enchanter Merlin and Sir Ulfius, and whence come they?" For all the world knew Merlin and Sir Ulfius, and they wist that here was something very extraordinary about to happen. And Arthur was clad all in flame-colored raiment embroidered with threads of silver, so that others of the people said, "Certes, that youth is very fair for to look upon; now who may he be?"

But Merlin said no word to any man, but he brought Arthur through the press unto that place where the Archbishop sat; and the press made way for him so that he was not stayed in his going. And when the Archbishop beheld Merlin come thus with those others, he arose and said, "Merlin, who are these whom thou bringest unto us, and what is their business here?" And Merlin said, "Lord, here is one come to make the assay of yonder sword." And the Archbishop said, "Which one is he?" and Merlin said, "This is he," and he laid his hand upon Arthur.

Then the Archbishop looked upon Arthur and he beheld that the youth was very comely of face, wherefore his heart went out unto Arthur and he loved him a very great deal. And the Archbishop said, "Merlin, by what right doth this young man come hither?" And Merlin made reply, "Lord, he cometh hither by the best right that there is in the world; for he who standeth before thee clad in red is the true son of Uther-Pendragon and of his lawful wife, Queen Igraine."

Then the Archbishop cried out aloud in great amazement and those who stood nigh and who heard what Merlin said were so astonished that they wist not what to think. And the Archbishop said, "Merlin, what is this that thou tellest me? For who, until now, in all the world hath ever heard that Uther-Pendragon had a son?"

Unto this Merlin made reply: "No one hath ever known of such a thing until now, only a very few. For it was in this wise: When this child was born the spirit of prophecy lay upon me and I foresaw that Uther-Pendragon would die before a very great while. Wherefore I feared that the enemies of the King would lay violent hands upon the young child for the sake of his inheritance. So, at the King's behest, I and another took the young child from his mother and gave him unto a third, and that man received the kingly child and maintained him ever since as his own son. And as to the truth of these things there are others here who may attest the verity of them—for he who was with me when the young

verity: Truth.

46

child was taken from his mother was Sir Ulfius, and he to whom he was entrusted was Sir Ector of Bonmaison—and those two witnesses, who are without any reproach, will avouch to the verity of that which I have asserted, for here they stand before thee to certify unto what I have said."

And Sir Ulfius and Sir Ector said, "All that Merlin hath spoken is true, and thereunto we do pledge our most faithful and sacred word of honor."

Then the Archbishop said, "Who is there may doubt the word of such honorable witnesses?" And he looked upon Arthur and smiled upon him.

Then Arthur said, "Have I then thy leave, Lord, to handle yonder sword?" And the Archbishop said, "Thou hast my leave, and may the grace of God go with thee to do thy endeavor."

Thereupon Arthur went to the cube of marble stone and he laid his hands upon the haft of the sword that was thrust into the anvil. And he bent his body and drew very strongly and, lo! the sword came forth with great ease and very smoothly. And when he had got the sword into his hands, he swung it about his head so that it flashed like lightning. And after he had swung it thus thrice about his head, he set the point thereof against the face of the anvil and bore upon it very strongly, and, behold! the sword slid very smoothly back again into that place where it had aforetime stood; and when it was there, midway deep, it stood fast where it was. And thus did Arthur successfully accomplish that marvellous miracle of the sword in the eyes of all the world.

aforetime: Previously.

Now when the people who were congregated at that place beheld this miracle performed before their faces, they lifted up their voices all together, and shouted so vehemently and with so huge a tumult of outcry that it was as though the whole earth rocked and trembled with the sound of their shouting.

tumult: A roar.

And whiles they so shouted Arthur took hold of the sword again and drew it forth and swung it again, and again drave it back into the anvil. And when he had done that he drew it forth a third time and did the same thing as before. Thus it was that all those who were there beheld that miracle performed three times over.

And all the kings and dukes who were there were filled with great amazement, and they wist not what to think or to say when they beheld one who was little more than a boy perform that undertaking in which the best of them had failed. And some of them, seeing that miracle, were willing to acknowledge Arthur because of it, but others would not acknowledge him. These withdrew themselves and stood aloof; and as they stood thus apart, they said among themselves: "What is this and who can accredit such a thing that a beardless boy should be set before us all and should be made King and overlord of this great realm for to govern us. Nay! nay! we will have none of him for our King." And others said, "Is it not apparent that Merlin and Sir Ulfius are thus exalting this unknown boy so that they may elevate themselves along with him?" Thus these discontented kings spake among themselves, and of all of them the most bitter were King Lot and King Urien, who were brothers by marriage with Arthur.

Now when the Archbishop perceived the discontent of these kings and dukes, he said to them, "How now, Messires! Are ye not satisfied?" And they said, "We are not satisfied." And the Archbishop said, "What would ye have?" And they said, "We would have another sort of king for Britain than a beardless boy of whom no one knoweth and of whose birthright there are only three men to attest." And the Archbishop said, "What of that? Hath he not performed the miracle that ye yourselves assayed and failed to perform?"

But these high and mighty lords would not be satisfied, but with angry and averted faces they went away from that place, filled with wrath and indignation.

But others of these kings and dukes came and saluted Arthur and paid him court, giving him joy of that which he had achieved; and the chiefest of those who came thus unto him in friendliness was King Leodegrance of Cameliard. And all the multitude acknowledged him and crowded around that place shouting so that it sounded like to the noise of thunder.

Now all this while Sir Ector and Sir Kay had stood upon one side. And they were greatly weighed down by sorrow; for it appeared to them that Arthur had, of a sudden, been uplifted so far from their estate that they might never hope to approach him more. For now he was of kingly consequence and they but common knights. And, after awhile, Arthur beheld them where they stood with downcast looks, whereupon he straightway went to them and took first one and then the other by the hand and kissed each upon the cheek. Thereupon they were again very glad at being thus uplifted unto him.

And when Arthur departed from that place, great crowds of people followed after him so that the streets were altogether filled with the press of people. And the multitude continually gave him loud acclaim as the chosen King of England, and those who were nearest to him sought to touch the hem of his garments; wherefore the heart of Arthur was exceedingly uplifted with great joy and gladness, so that his soul took wing and flew like a bird into the sky.

Thus Arthur achieved the adventure of the sword that day and entered into his birthright of royalty. Wherefore, may God grant His Grace unto you all that ye too may likewise succeed in your undertakings. For any man may be a king in that life in which he is placed if so be he may draw forth the sword of success from out of the iron of circumstance. Wherefore when your time of assay cometh, I do hope it may be with you as it was with Arthur that day, and that ye too may achieve success with entire satisfaction unto yourself and to your great glory and perfect happiness. Amen.

straightway: Here, immediately.

49

Conclusion

Now after these things had happened there was much talk among men and great confusion and tumult. For while some of the kings and nearly all the multitude said, "Lo! here is a king come to us, as it were, from out of Heaven for to bring peace unto our distracted land," yet other kings (and they were of greater number) said, "Who is this beardless boy who cometh with a claim to be High King of Britain? Who ever heard of him before? We will have none of him except upon further trial and upon greater avouchment." So, for the sake of peace, the Archbishop ordained that another assay of the sword should be made at Candlemas; and here again all those who endeavored to draw forth the sword failed thereat, but Arthur drew it forth several times, very easily, in the sight of all. And after that a third trial was made at Easter and after that a fourth trial was made at Pentecost. And at all these trials Arthur repeatedly drew out the sword from the anvil, and no one but he could draw it forth.

And, after that fourth trial, sundry of the kings and many of the lesser barons and knights and all of the commons cried out that these were trials enough, and that Arthur had

avouchment: Guarantee, proof.

sundry: Many different.

assuredly approved himself to be rightwise King; wherefore they demanded that he should be made King indeed so that he might rule over them. For it had come to pass that whithersoever Arthur went great crowds followed after him hailing him as the true son of Uther-Pendragon, and rightwise overlord of Britain. Wherefore, the Archbishop (seeing how the people loved Arthur and how greatly they desired him for their King) ordained that he should be anointed and crowned unto royal estate; and so it was done at the great Cathedral. And some say that that Cathedral was St. Paul's and some say that it was not.

But when Arthur had thus been crowned, all those who were opposed unto his Kingship withdrew themselves in great anger, and immediately set about to prepare war against him. But the people were with Arthur and joined with him, and so also did several Kings and many of the lesser barons and knights. And, with the advice of Merlin, Arthur made friends and allies of sundry other kings and they and he fought two great wars with his enemies and won both of these wars. And in the second war was fought a very famous battle nigh to the Forest of Bedegraine (wherefore it was called the Battle of Bedegraine), and in that battle Arthur overthrew his enemies so entirely that it was not possible for them ever to hope to unite in war against him again.

And of King Lot, his brother-in-law, King Arthur brought two of his sons to Court for to dwell there and to serve as hostages of peace thereafter. And these two were Gawaine and Geharris and they became, after awhile, very famous and accomplished knights. And of King Urien, his other brother-in-law, Arthur brought unto Court his one son, Ewaine, for to hold as an hostage of peace; and he also became in time a very famous and accomplished knight. And because of these hostages there was peace thereafter betwixt those three kingly brothers for all time. And a certain very famous king and knight hight King Pellinore (who was one of his enemies) Arthur drove out of his possessions and away from the habitations of men and into the forest. And King Ryence (who was another of his enemies) he drave into the mountains of North Wales. And other kings who were his enemies he subjugated to his will, so that all the land was at such peace that it had not enjoyed the like since the days of Uther-Pendragon.

And King Arthur made Sir Kay his Seneschal as he had promised to do; and he made Sir Ulfius his Chamberlain; and Merlin he made his Counsellor; and Sir Bodwain of Britain he made his Constable. And these men were all of such a sort as greatly enhanced the glory and renown of his reign and established him upon his throne with entire security.

Now when the reign of King Arthur became thus entirely established, and when the renown of his greatness began to be known in the world, many men of noble souls and of large spirit and of high knightly prowess—knights who desired above all things to achieve glory at arms in Courts of Chivalry—perceived that great credit and exaltation of estate were likely to be won under such a king. So it fell out that, from all parts, by little and little, there began to gather together such a Court of noble, honorable knights about King Arthur as men never beheld before that time, and shall haply never behold again.

For even to this day the history of these good knights is known to the greater part of mankind. Yea; the names of many kings and emperors have passed away and have been forgotten, but the names of Sir Galahad, and of Sir Launcelot of the Lake, and of Sir Tristram of Lyonesse, and of Sir Percival of Gales, and of Sir Gawaine, and of Sir Ewaine, and of Sir Bors de Ganis, and of many others of that noble household of worthy brotherhood, is still remembered by men. Wherefore, I think that it is very likely that so long as words shall be written, the performances of these worthies shall be remembered.

Chamberlain: Treasurer, the officer who receives the rents and revenues of the kingdom.

prowess: Courage, bravery.

So in this history yet to be written, I have set it for my task to inform him who reads this book of many of these adventures, telling him, besides, such several circumstances as I do not believe are known unto everybody. And by and by, when I shall tell of the establishment of the Round Table, I shall set forth a tabulated list of a number of those worthies who at this time assembled at the Court of Arthur as men chosen to found that order of the Round Table, and who, for that reason, were entitled "The Ancient and Honorable Companions of the Round Table."

For though this entire history chiefly concerneth King Arthur, yet the glory of these great honorable knights was his glory, and his glory was their glory, wherefore one cannot tell of the glory of King Arthur without also telling of the glory of those noble gentlemen aforesaid.

Part Two

The Winning of a Sword

Here beginneth the story of certain adventures of Arthur after that he had become King, wherein it is told how, with great knightly courage and prowess, he fought a very fierce and bloodly battle with a certain Sable Knight. Likewise, it is told how he achieved, in consequence of that battle, a certain Sword so famous and glorious that its renown shall last as long as our speech shall be spoken. For the like of that sword was never seen in all the world before that time, and it hath never been beheld since then; and its name was Excalibur.

So, if it please you to read this story, I believe it will afford you excellent entertainment, and will, without doubt, greatly exalt your spirit because of the remarkable courage which those two famous and worthy knights displayed when they fought together that famous battle. Likewise you shall find great cheer in reading therein of the wonderful marvellousness of a certain land of Faerie into which King Arthur wandered, and where he found a Lake of Enchantment and held converse with a mild and beautiful lady of that land who directed him how to obtain that renowned sword aforementioned.

held converse: Kept company.

For it hath given me such pleasure to write these things that my heart would, at times, be diluted as with a pure joy, wherefore, I entertain great hopes that you also may find much pleasure in them as I have already done. So I pray you to listen unto what follows.

diluted: Weakened.

Now it fell upon a certain pleasant time in the Springtide season that King Arthur and his Court were making a royal progression through that part of Britain which lieth close to the Forests of the Usk. At that time the weather was exceedingly warm, and so the King and Court made pause within the forest under the trees in the cool and pleasant shade that the place afforded, and there the King rested for a while upon a couch of rushes spread with scarlet cloth.

And the knights then present at that Court were, Sir Gawaine, and Sir Ewaine, and Sir Kay, and Sir Pellias, and Sir Bedevere, and Sir Caradoc, and Sir Geraint, and Sir Bodwin of Britain and Sir Constantine of Cornwall, and Sir Brandiles and Sir Mador de la Porte, and there was not to be found anywhere in the world a company of such noble and exalted knights as these.

Now as the King lay drowsing and as these worthies sat holding cheerful converse together at that place, there came, of a sudden, a considerable bustle and stir upon the outskirts

HOW THERE CAME A CERTAIN WOUNDED KNIGHT UNTO THE COURT OF KING ARTHUR, HOW A YOUNG KNIGHT OF THE KING'S COURT SOUGHT TO AVENGE HIM AND FAILED AND HOW THE KING THEREUPON TOOK THAT ASSAY UPON HIMSELF.

azure: Sky blue.

doleful: Sad.

succor: Here, aid and comfort.

chirurgeon: A doctor.

of the Court, and presently there appeared a very sad and woful sight. For there came thitherward a knight, sore wounded, and upheld upon his horse by a golden-haired page, clad in an apparel of white and azure. And, likewise, the knight's apparel and the trappings of his horse were of white and azure, and upon his shield he bore the emblazonment of a single lily flower of silver upon a ground of pure azure.

But the knight was in a very woful plight. For his face was as pale as wax and hung down upon his breast. And his eyes were glazed and saw naught that passed around him, and his fair apparel of white and blue was all red with the blood of life that ran from a great wound in his side. And, as they came upon their way, the young page lamented in such wise that it wrung the heart for to hear him.

Now, as these approached, King Arthur aroused cried out, "Alas! what doleful spectacle is that which I behold? Now hasten, ye my lords, and bring succor to yonder knight; and do thou, Sir Kay, go quickly and bring that fair young page hither that we may presently hear from his lips what mishap hath befallen his lord."

So certain of those knights hastened at the King's bidding and gave all succor to the wounded knight, and conveyed him to King Arthur's own pavilion, which had been pitched at a little distance. And when he had come there the King's chirurgeon presently attended upon him—albeit his wounds were of such a sort he might not hope to live for a very long while.

Meantime, Sir Kay brought that fair young page before the King, where he sat, and the King thought that he had hardly ever seen a more beautiful countenance. And the King said, "I prithee tell me, Sir Page, who is thy master, and how came he in such a sad and pitiable condition as that which we have just now beheld."

"That will I so, Lord," said the youth. "Know that my master is entitled Sir Myles of the White Fountain, and that he cometh from the country north of where we are and at a considerable distance from this. In that country he is the Lord of seven castles and several noble estates, wherefore, as thou mayst see, he is of considerable consequence. A fortnight ago (being doubtless moved thereunto by the lustiness of the Springtime), he set forth with only me for his esquire, for he had a mind to seek adventure in such manner as beseemed a good knight who would be errant. And we had several adventures, and in all of them my lord was entirely successful; for he overcame six knights at various places and sent them all to his castle for to attest his valor unto his lady.

"At last, this morning, coming to a certain place situated at a considerable distance from this, we came upon a fair castle of the forest, which stood in a valley surrounded by open spaces of level lawn, bedight with many flowers of divers sorts. There we beheld three fair damsels who tossed a golden ball from one to another, and the damsels were clad all in flame-colored satin, and their hair was of the color of gold. And as we drew nigh to them they stinted their play, and she who was the chief of those damsels called out to my lord, demanding of him whither he went and what was his errand.

"To her my lord made answer that he was errant and in search of adventure, and upon this, the three damsels laughed, and she who had first spoken said, 'An thou art in search of adventure, Sir Knight, happily I may be able to help thee to one that shall satisfy thee to thy heart's content.'

"Unto this my master made reply 'I prithee, fair damsel, tell me what that adventure may be so that I may presently assay it.'

"Thereupon this lady bade my master to take a certain path, and to follow the same for the distance of a league or a little more, and that he would then come to a bridge of stone that crossed a violent stream, and she assured him that there he might find adventure enough for to satisfy any man.

THE WINNING OF A SWORD

considerable consequence: Great importance.

bedight: Bedecked, ornamented, covered.

"So my master and I wended thitherward as that damoiselle had directed, and, by and by, we came unto the bridge whereof she had spoken. And, lo! beyond the bridge was a lonesome castle with a tall straight tower, and before the castle was a wide and level lawn of well-trimmed grass. And immediately beyond the bridge was an apple-tree hung over with a multitude of shields. And midway upon the bridge was a single shield, entirely of black; and beside it hung a hammer of brass; and beneath the shield was written these words in letters of red:

Whoso Smiteth This Shield
Doeth So At His Peril.

"Now, my master, Sir Myles, when he read those words went straightway to that shield and, seizing the hammer that hung beside it, he smote upon it a blow so that it rang like thunder.

"Thereupon, as in answer, the portcullis of the castle was let fall, and there immediately came forth a knight, clad all from head to foot in sable armor. And his apparel and the trappings of his horse and all the appointments thereof were likewise entirely of sable.

"Now when that Sable Knight perceived my master he came riding swiftly across the meadow and so to the other end of the bridge. And when he had come there he drew rein and saluted my master and cried out, 'Sir Knight, I demand of thee why thou didst smite that shield. Now let me tell thee, because of thy boldness, I shall take away from thee thine own shield, and shall hang it upon yonder apple-tree, where thou beholdest all those other shields to be hanging.' Unto this my master made reply. 'That thou shalt not do unless thou mayst overcome me, as knight to knight.' And thereupon, immediately, he dressed his shield and put himself into array for an assault at arms.

portcullis: A large, heavy iron grating moved by chains to admit or bar entrance to a castle.

60

"So my master and this Sable Knight, having made themselves ready for that encounter, presently drave together with might and main. And they met in the middle of the course, where my master's spear burst into splinters. But the spear of the Sable Knight held and it pierced through Sir Myles, his shield, and it penetrated his side, so that both he and his horse were overthrown violently into the dust; he being wounded so grievously that he could not arise again from the ground whereon he lay.

"Then the Sable Knight took my master's shield and hung it up in the branches of the apple-tree where the other shields were hanging, and, thereupon, without paying further heed to my master, or inquiring as to his hurt, he rode away into his castle again, whereof the portcullis was immediately closed behind him.

"So, after that he had gone, I got my master to his horse with great labor, and straightway took him thence, not knowing where I might find harborage for him, until I came to this place. And that, my lord King, is the true story of how my master came by that mortal hurt which he hath suffered."

"Ha! By the glory of Paradise!" cried King Arthur, "I do consider it great shame that in my Kingdom and so near to my Court strangers should be so discourteously treated as Sir Myles hath been served. For it is certainly a discourtesy for to leave a fallen knight upon the ground, without tarrying to inquire as to his hurt how grievous it may be. And still more discourteous is it for to take away the shield of a fallen knight who hath done good battle."

And so did all the knights of the King's Court exclaim against the discourtesy of that Sable Knight.

Then there came forth a certain esquire attendant upon the King's person, by name Griflet, who was much beloved by his Royal Master, and he kneeled before the King and cried out in a loud voice: "I crave a boon of thee, my lord

King! and do beseech thee that thou wilt grant it unto me!"

Then King Arthur uplifted his countenance upon the youth as he knelt before him and he said, "Ask, Griflet, and thy boon shall be granted unto thee."

Thereupon Griflet said, "It is this that I would ask—I crave that thou wilt make me straightway knight, and that thou wilt let me go forth and endeavor to punish this unkindly knight, by overthrowing him, and so redeeming those shields which he hath hung upon that apple-tree."

Then was King Arthur much troubled in his spirit, for Griflet was as yet only an esquire and altogether untried in arms. So he said, "Behold, thou art yet too young to have to do with so potent a knight as this sable champion must be, who has thus overthrown so many knights without himself suffering any mishap. I prithee, dear Griflet, consider and ask some other boon."

But young Griflet only cried the more, "A boon! A boon! and thou hast granted it unto me."

Thereupon King Arthur said, "Thou shalt have thy boon, though my heart much misgiveth me that thou wilt suffer great ill and misfortune from this adventure."

So that night Griflet kept watch upon his armor in a chapel of the forest, and, in the morning, having received the Sacrament, he was created a knight by the hand of King Arthur—and it was not possible for any knight to have greater honor than that. Then King Arthur fastened the golden spurs to Sir Griflet's heels with his own hand.

So Griflet was made a knight, and having mounted his charger, he rode straightway upon his adventure, much rejoicing and singing for pure pleasure.

And it was at this time that Sir Myles died of his hurt, for it is often so that death and misfortune befall some, whiles others laugh and sing for hope and joy, as though such grievous things as sorrow and death could never happen in the world wherein they live.

prithee: (I) Pray thee.

Prick Spurs

Now that afternoon King Arthur sat waiting with great
anxiety for word of that young knight, but there was no
word until toward evening, when there came hurrying to him
certain of his attendants, proclaiming that Sir Griflet was
returning, but without his shield, and in such guise that it
seemed as though a great misfortune had befallen him. And
straightway thereafter came Sir Griflet himself, sustained
upon his horse on the one hand by Sir Constantine and upon
the other by Sir Brandiles. And, lo! Sir Griflet's head hung
down upon his breast, and his fair new armor was all broken
and stained with blood and dust. And so woful was he of
appearance that King Arthur's heart was contracted with
sorrow to behold that young knight in so pitiable a
condition.

So, at King Arthur's bidding, they conducted Sir Griflet to the Royal Pavilion, and there they laid him down upon a soft couch. Then the King's chirurgeon searched his wounds and found that the head of a spear and a part of the shaft thereof were still piercing Sir Griflet's side, so that he was in most woful and grievous pain.

And when King Arthur beheld in what a parlous state Sir Griflet lay he cried out, "Alas! my dear young knight, what hath happened thee to bring thee unto such a woful condition as this which I behold?"

Then Sir Griflet, speaking in a very weak voice, told King Arthur how he had fared. And he said that he had proceeded through the forest, until he had discovered the three beautiful damsels whereof the page of Sir Myles had spoken. And he said that these damsels had directed him as to the manner in which he should pursue his adventure. And he said that he had found the bridge whereon hung the shield and the brazen mall, and that he had there beheld the apple-tree hung full of shields; and he said that he smote the shield of the Sable Knight with the brazen mall, and that the Sable Knight had thereupon come riding out against him. And he said that this knight did not appear of a mind to fight with him; instead, he cried out to him with a great deal of nobleness that he was too young and too untried in arms to have to do with a seasoned knight; wherefore he advised Sir Griflet to withdraw him from that adventure ere it was too late. But, notwithstanding this advice, Sir Griflet would not withdraw but declared that he would certainly have to do with that other knight in sable. Now at the very first onset Sir Griflet's spear had burst into pieces, but the spear of the Sable Knight had held and had pierced through Sir Griflet's shield and into his side, causing him this grievous wound whereof he suffered. And Sir Griflet said that the Sable Knight had then, most courteously, uplifted him upon his horse again (albeit he had kept Sir Griflet's shield and had hung it upon the tree with those others that hung there) and had then directed him upon his way, so that he had made shift to ride thither, though with great pain and dole.

Then was King Arthur very wode and greatly disturbed in his mind, for indeed he loved Sir Griflet exceedingly well. Wherefore he declared that he himself would now go forth for to punish that Sable Knight, and for to humble him with his own hand. And, though the knights of his Court strove to dissuade him from that adventure, yet he declared that he with his own hand would accomplish that proud knight's humiliation, and that he would undertake the adventure, with God His Grace, upon the very next day.

And so disturbed was he that he could scarce eat his food that evening for vexation, nor would he go to his couch to sleep, but, having inquired very narrowly of Sir Griflet where he might find that valley of flowers and those three damsels, he spent the night in walking up and down his pavilion, awaiting for the dawning of the day.

Now, as soon as the birds first began to chirp and the east to brighten with the coming of the daylight, King Arthur summoned his two esquires, and, having with their aid donned his armor and mounted a milk-white war-horse, he presently took his departure upon that adventure which he had determined upon.

And, indeed it is a very pleasant thing for to ride forth in the dawning of a Springtime day. For then the little birds do sing their sweetest song, all joining in one joyous medley, whereof one may scarce tell one note from another, so multitudinous is that pretty roundelay; then do the growing things of the earth smell the sweetest in the freshness of the early daytime—the fair flowers, the shrubs, and the blossoms upon the trees; then doth the dew bespangle all the sward as with an incredible multitude of jewels of various colors; then is all the world sweet and clean and new, as though it had been fresh created for him who came to roam abroad so early in the morning.

So King Arthur's heart expanded with great joy, and he

THE WINNING OF A SWORD

wode: Angry, furious.

roundelay: A song with a simple melody, like "Row, Row, Row Your Boat," that is repeated at various intervals. Roundelay is a good word to describe the rather chaotic way birds sing their songs.

sward: Grass-covered soil.

chanted a quaint song as he rode through the forest upon the quest of that knightly adventure.

So, about noon-tide, he came to that part of the forest lands whereof he had heard those several times before. For of a sudden, he discovered before him a wide and gently sloping valley, a-down which ran a stream as bright as silver. And, lo! the valley was strewn all over with an infinite multitude of fair and fragrant flowers of divers sorts. And in the midst of the valley there stood a comely castle, with tall red roofs and many bright windows, so that it seemed to King Arthur that it was a very fine castle indeed. And upon a smooth green lawn he perceived those three damoiselles clad in flame-colored satin of whom the page of Sir Myles and Sir Griflet had spoken. And they played at ball with a golden ball, and the hair of each was of the hue of gold, and it seemed to King Arthur, as he drew nigh, that they were the most beautiful damoiselles that he had ever beheld in all of his life.

Now as King Arthur came unto them the three ceased tossing the ball, and she who was the fairest of all damoiselles demanded of him whither he went and upon what errand he was bound.

Then King Arthur made reply: "Ha! fair lady! whither should a belted knight ride upon such a day as this, and upon what business, other than the search of adventure such as beseemeth a knight of a proper strength of heart and frame who would be errant?"

Then the three damoiselles smiled upon the King, for he was exceedingly comely of face and they liked him very well. "Alas, Sir Knight!" said she who had before spoken, "I prithee be in no such haste to undertake a dangerous adventure, but rather tarry with us for a day or two or three, for to feast and make merry with us. For surely good cheer doth greatly enlarge the heart, and we would fain enjoy the company of so gallant a knight as thou appearest to be. Yonder castle is ours and all this gay valley is ours, and those

damoiselles: A French word for damsels or maidens of gentle birth.

whither: Where.

tarry: Stay.

66

who have visited it are pleased, because of its joyousness, to call it the Valley of Delight. So tarry with us for a little and be not in such haste to go forward."

"Nay," said King Arthur, "I may not tarry with ye, fair ladies, for I am bent upon an adventure of which ye may wot right well, when I tell ye that I seek that Sable Knight, who hath overcome so many other knights and hath taken away their shields. So I do pray ye of your grace for to tell me where I may find him."

"Grace of Heaven!" cried she who spake for the others, "this is certainly a sorry adventure which ye seek, Sir Knight! For already, in these two days, have two knights assayed with that knight, and both have fallen into great pain and disregard. Ne'theless, an thou wilt undertake this peril, yet shalt thou not go until thou hast eaten and refreshed thyself." So saying, she lifted a little ivory whistle that hung from her neck by a chain of gold, and blew upon it very shrilly.

In answer to this summons there came forth from the castle three fair young pages, clad all in flame-colored raiment, bearing among them a silver table covered with a white napkin. And after them came five other pages of the same appearance, bearing flagons of white wine and red, dried fruits and comfits and manchets of white fair bread.

raiment: Clothing, attire.

comfits and manchets: Sugar-plums or sweetmeats.

Then King Arthur descended from his war-horse with great gladness, for he was both hungry and athirst, and, seating himself at the table with the damsels beside him, he ate with great enjoyment, discoursing pleasantly the while with those fair ladies, who listened to him with great cheerfulness of spirit. Yet he told them not who he was, though they greatly marvelled who might be the noble warrior who had come thus into that place.

So, having satisfied his hunger and his thirst, King Arthur mounted his steed again, and the three damsels conducted him across the valley a little way—he riding upon his horse and they walking beside him. So, by and by, he perceived where was a dark pathway that led into the farther side of the forest land; and when he had come thither the lady who had addressed him before said to him, "Yonder is the way that thou must take an thou wouldst enter upon this adventure. So fare thee well, and may good hap go with thee, for, certes, thou art the Knight most pleasant of address who hath come hitherward for this long time."

Thereupon King Arthur, having saluted those ladies right courteously, rode away with very great joy of that pleasant adventure through which he had thus passed.

Now when King Arthur had gone some ways he came, by and by, to a certain place where charcoal burners plied their trade. For here were many mounds of earth, all a-smoke with the smouldering logs within, whilst all the air was filled with the smell of the dampened fires.

As the King approached this spot, he presently beheld that something was toward that was sadly amiss. For, in the open clearing, he beheld three sooty fellows with long knives in their hands, who pursued one old man, whose beard was as white as snow. And he beheld that the reverend old man, who was clad richly in black, and whose horse stood at a little distance, was running hither and thither, as though to escape from those wicked men, and he appeared to be very hard pressed and in great danger of his life.

"Pardee!" quoth the young King to himself, "here, certes, is one in sore need of succor." Whereupon he cried out in a great voice, "Hold, villains! What would you be at!" and therewith set spurs to his horse and dropped his spear into rest and drove down upon them with a noise like to thunder for loudness.

But when the three wicked fellows beheld the armed Knight thus thundering down upon them, they straightway dropped their knives and, with loud outcries of fear, ran

toward: Happening.
amiss: Wrong, out of order.

reverend: Venerable, worthy of respect because of his age.

Pardee: An oath meaning verily, assuredly.

68

away hither and thither until they had escaped into the thickets of the forest, where one upon a horse might not hope to pursue them.

Whereupon, having driven away those wicked fellows, King Arthur rode up to him whom he had succored, thinking to offer him condolence. And behold! when he had come nigh to him, he perceived that the old man was the Enchanter Merlin. Yet whence he had so suddenly come, who had only a little while before been at the King's Court at Carleon, and what he did in that place, the King could in no wise understand. Wherefore he bespoke the Enchanter in this wise, "Ha! Merlin, it seemeth to me that I have saved thy life. For, surely, thou hadst not escaped from the hands of those wicked men had I not happened to come hitherward at this time."

"Dost thou think so, Lord?" said Merlin. "Now let me tell thee that I did maybe appear to be in danger, yet I might have saved myself very easily had I been of a mind to do so. But, as thou sawst me in this seeming peril, so may thou know that a real peril, far greater than this, lieth before thee, and there will be no errant knight to succor thee from it. Wherefore, I pray thee, Lord, for to take me with thee upon this adventure that thou art set upon, for I do tell thee that thou shalt certainly suffer great dole and pain therein."

"Merlin," said King Arthur, "even an I were to face my death, yet would I not turn back from this adventure. But touching the advice thou givest me, meseems it will be very well to take thee with me if such peril lieth before me as thou sayest."

And Merlin said, "Yea, it would be very well for thee to do so."

So Merlin mounted upon his palfrey, and King Arthur and he betook their way from that place in pursuit of that adventure which the King had undertaken to perform.

succored: Here, rescued.

meseems: It seems to me; I think.

palfrey: A gentle riding horse that is smaller than the knight's cumbersome war horse.

So King Arthur and Merlin rode together through the forest for a considerable while, until they perceived that they must be approaching nigh to the place where dwelt the Sable Knight whom the King sought so diligently. For the forest, which had till then been altogether a wilderness, very deep and mossy, began to show an aspect more thin and open, as though a dwelling-place of mankind was close at hand.

And, after a little, they beheld before them a violent stream of water, that rushed through a dark and dismal glen. And, likewise, they perceived that across this stream of water there was a bridge of stone, and that upon the other side of the bridge there was a smooth and level lawn of green grass, whereon Knights-contestants might joust very well. And beyond this lawn they beheld a tall and forbidding castle, with smooth walls and a straight tower; and this castle was built upon the rocks so that it appeared to be altogether a part of the stone. So they wist that this must be the castle whereof the page and Sir Griflet had spoken.

For, midway upon the bridge, they beheld that there hung a sable shield and a brass mall exactly as the page and Sir Griflet had said; and that upon the farther side of the stream was an apple-tree, amid the leaves of which hung a very great many shields of various devices, exactly as those two had reported: and they beheld that some of those shields were

2

HOW KING ARTHUR FOUGHT WITH THE SABLE KNIGHT AND HOW HE WAS SORELY WOUNDED. LIKEWISE HOW MERLIN BROUGHT HIM SAFE AWAY FROM THE FIELD OF BATTLE.

clean and fair, and that some were foul and stained with blood, and that some were smooth and unbroken, and that some were cleft as though by battle of knight with knight. And all those shields were the shields of different knights whom the Sable Knight, who dwelt within the castle, had overthrown in combat with his own hand.

"Splendor of Paradise!" quoth King Arthur, "that must, indeed, be a right valiant knight who, with his own single strength, hath overthrown and cast down so many other knights. For, indeed, Merlin, there must be an hundred shields hanging in yonder tree!"

Unto this Merlin made reply, "And thou, Lord, mayst be very happy an thy shield, too, hangeth not there ere the sun goeth down this even-tide."

"That," said King Arthur, with a very steadfast countenance, "shall be as God willeth. For, certes, I have a greater mind than ever for to try my power against yonder knight. For, consider, what especial honor would fall to me should I overcome so valiant a warrior as this same Sable Champion appeareth to be, seeing that he hath been victorious over so many other good knights."

Thereupon, having so spoken his mind, King Arthur immediately pushed forward his horse and so, coming upon the bridge, he clearly read that challenge writ in letters of red beneath the shield:

Whoso Smiteth This Shield
Doeth So At His Peril.

Upon reading these words, the King seized the brazen mall, and smote that shield so violent a blow that the sound thereof echoed back from the smooth walls of the castle, and from the rocks whereon it stood, and from the skirts of the forest around about, as though twelve other shields had been struck in those several places.

And in answer to that sound, the portcullis of the castle

was immediately let fall, and there issued forth a knight, very huge of frame, and clad all in sable armor. And, likewise, all of his apparel and all the trappings of his horse were entirely of sable, so that he presented a most grim and forbidding aspect. And this Sable Knight came across that level meadow of smooth grass with a very stately and honorable gait; for neither did he ride in haste, nor did he ride slowly, but with great pride and haughtiness of mien, as became a champion who, haply, had never yet been overcome in battle. So, reaching the bridge-head, he drew rein and saluted King Arthur with great dignity, and also right haughtily. "Ha! Sir Knight!" quoth he, "why didst thou, having read those words yonder inscribed, smite upon my shield? Now I do tell thee that, for thy discourtesy, I shall presently take thy shield away from thee, and shall hang it up upon yonder apple-tree where thou beholdest all those other shields to be hanging. Wherefore, either deliver thou thy shield unto me without more ado or else prepare for to defend it with thy person—in the which event thou shalt certainly suffer great pain and discomfort to thy body."

"Gramercy for the choice thou grantest me," said King Arthur. "But as for taking away my shield—I do believe that that shall be as Heaven willeth, and not as thou willest. Know, thou unkind knight, that I have come hither for no other purpose than to do battle with thee and so to endeavor for to redeem with my person all those shields that hang yonder upon that apple-tree. So make thou ready straightway that I may have to do with thee, maybe to thy great disadvantage."

"That will I so," replied the Sable Knight. And thereupon he turned his horse's head and, riding back a certain distance across the level lawn, he took stand in such place as appeared to him to be convenient. And so did King Arthur ride forth also upon that lawn, and take his station as seemed to him to be convenient.

Then each knight dressed his spear and his shield for the

haughtiness of mien: In an arrogant manner.

ado: Needless trouble.

Gramercy: Thank you.

Guard

Truncheon

encounter, and, having thus made ready for the assault, each shouted to his war-horse and drave his spurs deep into its flank.

Then those two noble steeds rushed forth like lightning, coursing across the ground with such violent speed that the earth trembled and shook beneath them, an it were by cause of an earthquake. So those two knights met fairly in the midst of the centre of the field, crashing together like a thunderbolt. And so violently did they smite the one against the other that the spears burst into splinters, even unto the guard and the truncheon thereof, and the horses of the riders staggered back from the onset, so that only because of the extraordinary address of the knights-rider did they recover from falling before that shock of meeting.

But, with great spirit, these two knights uplifted each his horse with his own spirit, and so completed his course in safety.

And indeed King Arthur was very much amazed that he had not overthrown his opponent, for, at that time as aforesaid, he was considered to be the very best knight and the one best approved in deeds of arms that lived in all of Britain. Wherefore he marvelled at the power and the address of that knight against whom he had driven, that he had not been overthrown by the greatness of the blow that had been delivered against his defences. So, when they met again in the midst of the field, King Arthur gave that knight greeting, and bespoke him with great courtesy, addressing him in this wise: "Sir Knight, I know not who thou art, but I do pledge my knightly word that thou art the most potent knight that ever I have met in all of my life. Now I do bid thee get down straightway from thy horse, and let us two fight this battle with sword and upon foot, for it were pity to let it end in this way."

"Not so," quoth the Sable Knight—"not so, nor until one of us twain be overthrown will I so contest this battle upon foot." And upon this he shouted, "Ho! Ho!" in a very loud voice, and straightway thereupon the gateway of the castle opened and there came running forth two tall esquires clad all in black, pied with crimson. And each of these esquires bare in his hand a great spear of ash-wood, new and well-seasoned, and never yet strained in battle.

So King Arthur chose one of these spears and the Sable Knight took the other, and thereupon each returned to that station wherefrom he had before essayed the encounter.

Then once again each knight rushed his steed to the assault, and once again did each smite so fairly in the midst of the defence of the other that the spears were splintered, so that only the guard and the truncheon thereof remained in the grasp of the knight who held it.

Then, as before, King Arthur would have fought the battle out with swords and upon foot, but again the Sable Knight would not have it so, but called aloud upon those within the castle, whereupon there immediately came forth two other esquires with fresh, new spears of ash-wood. So each knight again took him a spear, and having armed himself therewith, chose each his station upon that fair, level lawn of grass.

And now, for the third time, having thus prepared themselves thereof assault, those two excellent knights hurled themselves together in furious assault. And now, as twice before, did King Arthur strike the Sable Knight so fairly in the centre of his defence that the spear which he held was burst into splinters. But this time, the spear of the Sable Knight did not so break in that manner, but held; and so violent was the blow that he delivered upon King Arthur's shield that he pierced through the centre of it. Then the girths of the King's saddle burst apart by that great, powerful blow, and both he and his steed were cast violently backward. So King Arthur might have been overcast, had he not voided his saddle with extraordinary skill and knightly address, wherefore, though his horse was overthrown, he himself still held his footing and did not fall into the dust. Ne'theless, so violent was the blow that he received that, for

pied: Partly colored.

girths: The leather bands holding a saddle on a horse.

voided his saddle: Dismounted.

75

a little space, he was altogether bereft of his senses so that everything whirled around before his eyes.

But when his sight returned to him he was filled with an anger so vehement that it appeared to him as though all the blood in his heart rushed into his brains so that he saw naught but red, as of blood, before his eyes. And when this also had passed he perceived the Sable Knight that he sat his horse at no great distance. Then immediately King Arthur ran to him and catching the bridle-rein of his horse, he cried out aloud unto that Sable Knight with great violence: "Come down, thou black knight! and fight me upon foot and with thy sword."

"That will I not do," said the Sable Knight, "for lo! I have overthrown thee. Wherefore deliver thou to me thy shield, that I may hang it upon yonder apple-tree, and go thy way as others have done before thee."

"That will I not!" cried King Arthur, with exceeding passion, "neither will I yield myself nor go hence until either thou or I have altogether conquered the other." Thereupon he thrust the horse of the Sable Knight backward by the bridle-rein so vehemently, that the other was constrained to void his saddle to save himself from being overthrown upon the ground.

And now each knight was as entirely furious as the other, wherefore, each drew his sword and dressed his shield, and thereupon rushed together like two wild bulls in battle. They foined, they smote, they traced, they parried, they struck again and again, and the sound of their blows, crashing and clashing the one upon the other, filled the entire surrounding space with an extraordinary uproar. Nor may any man altogether conceive of the entire fury of that encounter, for, because of the violence of the blows which the one delivered upon the other, whole cantels of armor were hewn from their bodies and many deep and grievous wounds were given and received, so that the armor of each was altogether stained with red because of the blood that flowed down upon it.

vehemently: Here, violently.

foined: Lunged, stabbed at.

At last King Arthur, waxing, as it were, entirely mad, struck so fierce a blow that no armor could have withstood that stroke had it fallen fairly upon it. But it befell with that stroke that his sword broke at the hilt and the blade thereof flew into three several pieces into the air. Yet was the stroke so wonderfully fierce that the Sable Knight groaned, and staggered, and ran about in a circle as though he had gone blind and knew not whither to direct his steps.

waxing: Becoming.

But presently he recovered himself again, and perceiving King Arthur standing near by, and not knowing that his enemy had now no sword for to defend himself withal, he cast aside his shield and took his own sword into both hands, and therewith smote so dolorous a stroke that he clave through King Arthur's shield and through his helmet and even to the bone of his brain-pan.

Then King Arthur thought that he had received his death-wound, for his brains swam like water, his thighs trembled exceedingly, and he sank down to his knees, whilst the blood and sweat, commingled together in the darkness of his helmet, flowed down into his eyes in a lather and blinded him. Thereupon, seeing him thus grievously hurt, the Sable Knight called upon him with great vehemence for to yield himself and to surrender his shield, because he was now too sorely wounded for to fight any more.

But King Arthur would not yield himself, but catching the other by the sword-belt, he lifted himself to his feet. Then, being in a manner recovered from his amazement, he embraced the other with both arms, and placing his knee behind the thigh of the Sable Knight, he cast him backward down upon the ground so violently that the sound of the fall was astounding to hear. And with that fall the Sable Knight was, awhile, entirely bereft of consciousness. Then King Arthur straightway unlaced the helm of the Sable Knight and so beheld his face, and he knew him in spite of the blood that still ran down his own countenance in great quantities, and he knew that knight was King Pellinore, aforenamed in this history, who had twice warred against King Arthur. (It hath already been said how King Arthur had driven that other king from the habitations of men and into the forests, so that now he dwelt in this poor gloomy castle whence he waged war against all the knights who came unto that place.)

Now when King Arthur beheld whom it was against whom he had done battle, he cried out aloud, "Ha! Pellinore, is it

commingled: Mixed.

bereft of: Deprived of, without.

habitations: Homes.

then thou? Now yield thee to me, for thou art entirely at my mercy." And upon this he drew his misericordia and set the point thereof at King Pellinore's throat.

But by now King Pellinore had greatly recovered from his fall, and perceiving that the blood was flowing down in great measure from out his enemy's helmet, he wist that that other must have been very sorely wounded by the blow which he had just now received. Wherefore he catched King Arthur's wrist in his hand and directed the point of the dagger away from his own throat so that no great danger threatened therefrom.

And, indeed, what with his sore wound and with the loss of blood, King Arthur was now fallen exceedingly sick and faint, so that it appeared to him that he was nigh to death. Accordingly, it was with no very great ado that King Pellinore suddenly heaved himself up from the ground and so overthrew his enemy that King Arthur was now underneath his knees.

And by this King Pellinore was exceedingly mad with the fury of the sore battle he had fought. For he was so enraged that his eyes were all beshot with blood like those of a wild boar, and a froth, like the champings of a wild boar, stood in the beard about his lips. Wherefore he wrenched the dagger out of his enemy's hand, and immediately began to unlace his helm, with intent to slay him where he lay. But at this moment Merlin came in great haste, crying out, "Stay! stay! Sir Pellinore; what would you be at? Stay your sacrilegious hand! For he who lieth beneath you is none other than Arthur, King of all this realm!"

At this King Pellinore was astonished beyond measure. And for a little he was silent, and then after a while he cried out in a very loud voice, "Say you so, old man? Then verily your words have doomed this man unto death. For no one in all this world hath ever suffered such ill and such wrongs as I have suffered at his hands. For, lo! he hath taken from me

THE WINNING OF A SWORD

misericordia: A slender dagger used to give the death stroke to a mortally wounded knight.

Wild Boar

Stay your sacrilegious hand!: This cry is at once an appeal and a warning, for if Sir Pellinore does not stop his hand, he will commit an unholy deed.

abiding-place: A home; quarters.

power, and kingship, and honors, and estates, and hath left me only this gloomy, dismal castle of the forest as an abiding-place. Wherefore, seeing that he is thus in my power, he shall now presently die; if for no other reason than because if I now let him go free, he will certainly revenge himself when he shall have recovered from all the ill he hath suffered at my hands."

Then Merlin said, "Not so! He shall not die at thy hands, for I, myself, shall save him." Whereupon he uplifted his staff and smote King Pellinore across the shoulders. Then immediately King Pellinore fell down and lay upon the ground on his face like one who had suddenly gone dead.

Upon this, King Arthur uplifted himself upon his elbow and beheld his enemy lying there as though dead, and he cried out, "Ha! Merlin! what is this that thou hast done? I am very sorry, for I do perceive that thou, by thy arts of magic, hath slain one of the best knights in all the world."

"Not so, my lord King!" said Merlin; "for, in sooth, I tell thee that thou art far nigher to thy death than he. For he is but in sleep and will soon awaken; but thou art in such a case that it would take only a very little for to cause thee to die."

And indeed King Arthur was exceeding sick, even to the heart, with the sore wound he had received, so that it was only with much ado that Merlin could help him up upon his horse. Having done the which and having hung the King's shield upon the horn of his saddle, Merlin straightway conveyed the wounded man thence across the bridge, and, leading the horse by the bridle, so took him away into the forest.

sore: Serious.

Now I must tell you that there was in that part of the forest a certain hermit so holy that the wild birds of the woodland would come and rest upon his hand whiles he read his breviary; and so sanctified was he in gentleness that the wild does would come even to the door of his hermitage, and there stand whilst he milked them for his refreshment. And

breviary: A book containing daily prayers.

this hermit dwelt in that part of the forest so remote from the habitations of man that when he rang the bell for matins or for vespers, there was hardly ever anyone to hear the sound thereof excepting the wild creatures that dwelt thereabout. Yet, ne'theless, to this remote and lonely place royal folk and others of high degree would sometimes come, as though on a pilgrimage, because of the hermit's exceeding saintliness.

So Merlin conveyed King Arthur unto this sanctuary, and, having reached that place, he and the hermit lifted the wounded man down from his saddle—the hermit giving many words of pity and sorrow—and together they conveyed him into the holy man's cell. There they laid him upon a couch of moss and unlaced his armor and searched his wounds and bathed them with pure water and dressed his hurts, for that hermit was a very skilful leech. So for all that day and part of the next, King Arthur lay upon the hermit's pallet like one about to die; for he beheld all things about him as though through thin water, and the breath hung upon his lips and fluttered, and he could not even lift his head from the pallet because of the weakness that lay upon him.

Now upon the afternoon of the second day there fell a great noise and tumult in that part of the forest. For it happened that the Lady Guinevere of Cameliard, together with her Court, both of ladies and of knights, had come upon a pilgrimage to that holy man, the fame of whose saintliness had reached even unto the place where she dwelt. For that lady had a favorite page who was very sick of a fever, and she trusted that the holy man might give her some charm or amulet by the virtue of which he might haply be cured. Wherefore she had come to that place with her entire Court so that all that part of the forest was made gay with fine raiment and the silence thereof was made merry with the sound of talk and laughter and the singing of songs and the chattering of many voices and the neighing of horses. And

THE WINNING OF A SWORD

matins. . .vespers: Morning and evening prayer services.

hermit's. . .saintliness: Many hermits in Medieval England were monks who went into the wilderness to be close to God and nature.

leech: One who used leeches to draw blood from the ill. Until fairly recent times, it was believed that such bleeding would cure illness.
pallet: A small, hard inferior bed. Certainly a couch of moss would qualify as a pallet.

amulet: A charm to bring good fortune. The top amulet shown is from the Vatican collection; the lower from a private collection.

the Lady Guinevere rode in the midst of her damsels and her Court, and her beauty outshone the beauty of her damsels as the splendor of the morning star outshines that of all the lesser stars that surround it. For then and afterward she was held by all the Courts of Chivalry to be the most beautiful lady in the world.

Now when the Lady Guinevere had come to that place, she perceived the milk-white war-horse of King Arthur where it stood cropping the green grass of the open glade nigh to the hermitage. And likewise she perceived Merlin, where he stood beside the door of the cell. So of him she demanded whose was that noble war-horse that stood browsing upon the grass at that lonely place, and who was it that lay within that cell. And unto her Merlin made answer, "Lady, he who lieth within is a knight, very sorely wounded, so that he is sick nigh unto death!"

"Pity of Heaven!" cried the Lady Guinevere. "What a sad thing is this that thou tellest me! Now I do beseech thee to lead me presently unto that knight that I may behold him. For I have in my Court a very skilful leech, who is well used to the cure of hurts such as knights receive in battle."

So Merlin brought the lady into the cell, and there she beheld King Arthur where he lay stretched upon the pallet. And she wist not who he was. Yet it appeared to her that in all her life she had not beheld so noble appearing a knight as he who lay sorely wounded in that lonely place. And King Arthur cast his looks upward to where she stood beside his bed of pain, surrounded by her maidens, and in the great weakness that lay upon him he wist not whether she whom he beheld was a mortal lady or whether she was not rather some tall straight angel who had descended from one of the Lordly Courts of Paradise for to visit him in his pain and distresses. And the Lady Guinevere was filled with a great pity at beholding King Arthur's sorrowful estate. Wherefore she called to her that skilful leech who was with her Court.

browsing: Grazing.

82

And she bade him bring a certain alabaster box of exceedingly precious balsam. And she commanded him for to search that knight's wounds and to anoint them with the balsam, so that he might be healed of his hurts with all despatch.

So that wise and skilful leech did according to the Lady Guinevere's commands, and immediately King Arthur felt entire ease of all his aches and great content of spirit. And when the Lady and her Court had departed, he found himself much uplifted in heart, and three days thereafter he was entirely healed and was as well and strong and lusty as ever he had been in all of his life.

And this was the first time that King Arthur ever beheld that beautiful lady, the Lady Guinevere of Cameliard, and from that time forth he never forgot her, but she was almost always present in his thoughts. Wherefore, when he was recovered he said thus to himself: "I will forget that I am a king and I will cherish the thought of this lady and will serve her faithfully as a good knight may serve his chosen dame."

And so he did, as ye shall hear later in this book.

alabaster. . .balsam: Alabaster is a hard, light-colored material resembling marble. Balsam could be any sort of healing potion.

ow, as soon as King Arthur had, by means of that extraordinary balsam, been thus healed of those grievous wounds which he had received in his battle with King Pellinore, he found himself to be moved by a most vehement desire to meet his enemy again for to try issue of battle with him once more, and so recover the credit which he had lost in that combat. Now, upon the morning of the fourth day, being entirely cured, and having broken his fast, he walked for refreshment beside the skirts of the forest, listening the while to the cheerful sound of the wood-birds singing their matins, all with might and main. And Merlin walked beside him, and King Arthur spake his mind to Merlin concerning his intent to engage once more in knightly contest with King Pellinore. And he said, "Merlin, it doth vex me very sorely for to have come off so ill in my late encounter with king Pellinore. Certes, he is the very best knight in all the world whom I have ever yet encountered. Ne'theless, it might have fared differently with me had I not broken my sword, and so left myself altogether defenceless in that respect. Howsoever that may be, I am of a mind for to assay this adventure once more, and so will I do as immediately as may be."

Thereunto Merlin made reply, "Thou art, assuredly, a very brave man to have so much appetite for battle, seeing how

3

HOW KING ARTHUR FOUND A NOBLE SWORD IN A VERY WONDERFUL MAN-NER. AND HOW HE AGAIN FOUGHT WITH IT AND WON THAT BATTLE.

skirts: The borders, edges, outer limits.

nigh thou camest unto thy death not even four days ago. Yet how mayst thou hope to undertake this adventure without due preparation? For, lo! thou hast no sword, nor hast thou a spear, nor hast thou even thy misericordia for to do battle withal. How then mayst thou hope for to assay this adventure?"

And King Arthur said, "That I know not, nevertheless I will presently seek for some weapon as soon as may be. For, even an I have no better weapon than an oaken cudgel, yet would I assay this battle again with so poor a tool as that."

oaken cudgel: An oak club.

"Ha! Lord," said Merlin, "I do perceive that thou art altogether fixed in thy purpose for to renew this quarrel. Wherefore, I will not seek to stay thee therefrom, but will do all that in me lies for to aid thee in thy desires. Now to this end I must tell thee that in one part of this forest (which is, indeed, a very strange place) there is a certain woodland sometimes called Arroy, and other times called the Forest of Adventure. For no knight ever entereth therein but some adventure befalleth him. And close to Arroy is a land of enchantment which has several times been seen. And that is a very wonderful land, for there is in it a wide and considerable lake, which is also of enchantment. And in the centre of that lake there hath for some time been seen the appearance as of a woman's arm—exceedingly beautiful and clad in white samite, and the hand of this arm holdeth a sword of such exceeding excellence and beauty that no eye hath ever beheld its like. And the name of this sword is Excalibur—it being so named by those who have beheld it because of its marvellous brightness and beauty. For it hath come to pass that several knights have already seen that sword and have endeavored to obtain it for their own, but, heretofore, no one hath been able to touch it, and many have lost their lives in that adventure. For when any man draweth near unto it, either he sinks into the lake, or else the arm disappeareth entirely, or else it is withdrawn beneath the lake; wherefore no man hath ever been able to obtain the possession of that sword. Now I

samite: A rich, heavy silk fabric.

am able to conduct thee unto that Lake of Enchantment, and there thou mayst see Excalibur with thine own eyes. Then when thou hast seen him thou mayst, haply, have the desire to obtain him; which, an thou art able to do, thou wilt have a sword very fitted for to do battle with."

"Merlin," quoth the king, "this is a very strange thing which thou tellest me. Now I am desirous beyond measure for to attempt to obtain this sword for mine own, wherefore I do beseech thee to lead me with all despatch to this enchanted lake whereof thou tellest me." And Merlin said, "I will do so."

So that morning King Arthur and Merlin took leave of that holy hermit (the King having kneeled in the grass to receive his benediction), and so, departing from that place, they entered the deeper forest once more, betaking their way to that part which was known as Arroy.

And after awhile they came to Arroy, and it was about noon-tide. And when they had entered into those woodlands they came to a certain little open place, and in that place they beheld a white doe with a golden collar about its neck. And King Arthur said, "Look, Merlin, yonder is a wonderful sight." And Merlin said, "Let us follow that doe." And upon this the doe turned and they followed it. And by and by in following it they came to an opening in the trees where was a little lawn of sweet soft grass. Here they beheld a bower and before the bower was a table spread with a fair snow-white cloth, and set with refreshments of white bread, wine, and meats of several sorts. And at the door of this bower there stood a page, clad all in green, and his hair was as black as ebony, and his eyes as black as jet and exceeding bright. And when this page beheld King Arthur and Merlin, he gave them greeting, and welcomed the King very pleasantly saying, "Ha! King Arthur, thou art welcome to this place. Now I prithee dismount and refresh thyself before going farther."

Then was King Arthur a-doubt as to whether there might not be some enchantment in this for to work him an ill, for

bower: A shady retreat enclosed by overhanging boughs.

goblets: Large, sometimes richly engraved, pewter, silver, or gold glasses used by royalty. Today, any glass with a base and stem is called a goblet.

he was astonished that that page in the deep forest should know him so well. But Merlin bade him have good cheer, and he said, "Indeed, Lord, thou mayst freely partake of that refreshment which, I may tell thee, was prepared especially for thee. Moreover in this thou mayst foretell a very happy issue unto this adventure."

So King Arthur sat down to the table with great comfort of heart (for he was an hungered) and that page and another like unto him·ministered unto his needs, serving him all the food upon silver plates, and all the wine in golden goblets as he was used to being served in his own court—only that those things were much more cunningly wrought and fashioned, and were more beautiful than the table furniture of the King's court.

Then, after he had eaten his fill and had washed his hands from a silver basin which the first page offered to him, and had wiped his hands upon a fine linen napkin which the other page brought unto him, and after Merlin had also refreshed himself, they went their way, greatly rejoicing at this pleasant adventure, which, it seemed to the King, could not but betoken a very good issue to his undertaking.

Now about the middle of the afternoon King Arthur and Merlin came, of a sudden, out from the forest and upon a fair and level plain, bedight all over with such a number of flowers that no man could conceive of their quantity nor of the beauty thereof.

And this was a very wonderful land, for, lo! all the air appeared as it were to be as of gold—so bright was it and so singularly radiant. And here and there upon that plain were sundry trees all in blossom; and the fragrance of the blossoms was so sweet that the King had never smelt any fragrance like to it. And in the branches of those trees were a multitude of birds of many colors, and the melody of their singing ravished the heart of the hearer. And midway in the plain was a lake of water as bright as silver, and all around the borders of the lake were incredible numbers of lilies and of daffodils. Yet, although this place was so exceedingly fair, there was, nevertheless, nowhere about it a single sign of human life of any sort, but it appeared altogether as lonely as the hollow sky upon a day of summer. So, because of all the marvellous beauty of this place, and because of its strangeness and its entire solitude, King Arthur perceived that he must have come into a land of powerful enchantment where, happily, dwelt a fairy of very exalted quality; wherefore his spirit was enwrapped in a manner of fear, as he pushed his great milk-white war-horse through that long fair grass, all bedight with flowers, and he wist not what strange things were about to befall him.

So when he had come unto the margin of the lake he beheld there the miracle that Merlin had told him of aforetime. For, lo! in the midst of the expanse of water there was the appearance of a fair and beautiful arm, as of a woman, clad all in white samite. And the arm was encircled with several bracelets of wrought gold; and the hand held a sword of marvellous workmanship aloft in the air above the surface of the water; and neither the arm nor the sword moved so much as a hair's-breadth, but were motionless like to a carven image upon the surface of the lake. And, behold! the sun of that strange land shone down upon the hilt of the sword, and it was of pure gold beset with jewels of several sorts, so that the hilt of the sword and the bracelets that encircled the arm glistered in the midst of the lake like to some singular star of exceeding splendor. And King Arthur sat upon his war-horse and gazed from a distance at the arm and the sword, and he greatly marvelled thereat; yet he wist not how he might come at that sword, for the lake was wonderfully wide and deep, wherefore he knew not how he might come thereunto for to make it his own. And as he sat pondering this thing within himself, he was suddenly aware of a strange lady, who approached him through those tall flowers that bloomed along the margin of the lake. And when

he perceived her coming toward him he quickly dismounted
from his war-horse and he went forward for to meet her with
the bridle-rein over his arm. And when he had come nigh to
her, he perceived that she was extraordinarily beautiful, and
that her face was like wax for clearness, and that her eyes
were perfectly black, and that they were as bright and
glistening as though they were two jewels set in ivory. And he
perceived that her hair was like silk and as black as it was
possible to be, and so long that it reached unto the ground as
she walked. And the lady was clad all in green—only that a
fine cord of crimson and gold was interwoven into the plaits
of her hair. And around her neck there hung a very beautiful
necklace of several strands of opal stones and emeralds, set in
cunningly wrought gold; and around her wrists were bracelets
of the like sort—of opal stones and emeralds set into gold. So
when King Arthur beheld her wonderful appearance, that it
was like to an ivory statue of exceeding beauty clad all in
green, he immediately kneeled before her in the midst of all
those flowers as he said, "Lady, I do certainly perceive that
thou art no mortal damoiselle, but that thou art Fay. Also
that this place, because of its extraordinary beauty, can be no
other than some land of Faerie into which I have entered."

And the Lady replied, "King Arthur, thou sayest soothly,
for I am indeed Faerie. Moreover, I may tell thee that my
name is Nymue, and that I am the chiefest of those Ladies of
the Lake of whom thou mayst have heard people speak. Also
thou art to know that what thou beholdest yonder as a wide
lake is, in truth, a plain like unto this, all bedight with
flowers. And likewise thou art to know that in the midst of
that plain there standeth a castle of white marble and of
ultramarine illuminated with gold. But, lest mortal eyes
should behold our dwelling-place, my sisters and I have
caused it to be that this appearance as of a lake should
extend all over that castle so that it is entirely hidden from
sight. Nor may any mortal man cross that lake, saving in one
way—otherwise he shall certainly perish therein."

90

"Lady," said King Arthur, "that which thou tellest me causes me to wonder a very great deal. And, indeed, I am afraid that in coming hitherward I have been doing amiss for to intrude upon the solitude of your dwelling-place."

"Nay, not so, King Arthur," said the Lady of the Lake, "for, in truth, thou art very welcome hereunto. Moreover, I may tell thee that I have a greater friendliness for thee and those noble knights of thy court than thou canst easily wot of. But I do beseech thee of thy courtesy for to tell me what it is that brings thee to our land?"

"Lady," quoth the King, "I will tell thee the entire truth. I fought of late a battle with a certain sable knight, in the which I was sorely and grievously wounded, and wherein I burst my spear and snapped my sword and lost even my misericordia, so that I had not a single thing left me by way of a weapon. In this extremity Merlin, here, told me of Excalibur, and of how he is continually upheld by an arm in the midst of this magical lake. So I came hither and, behold, I find it even as he hath said. Now, Lady, an it be possible, I would fain achieve that excellent sword, that, by means of it I might fight my battle to its entire end."

"Ha! my lord King," said the Lady of the Lake, "that sword is no easy thing for to achieve, and, moreover, I may tell thee that several knights have lost their lives by attempting that which thou hast a mind to do. For, in sooth, no man may win yonder sword unless he be without fear and without reproach."

"Alas, Lady!" quoth King Arthur, "that is indeed a sad saying for me. For, though I may not lack in knightly courage, yet, in truth, there be many things wherewith I do reproach myself withal. Ne'theless, I would fain attempt this thing, even an it be to my great endangerment. Wherefore, I prithee tell me how I may best undertake this adventure."

"King Arthur," said the Lady of the Lake, "I will do what I say to aid thee in thy wishes in this matter." Whereupon she lifted a single emerald that hung by a small chain of gold at her girdle and, lo! the emerald was cunningly carved into the form of a whistle. And she set the whistle to her lips and blew upon it very shrilly. Then straightway there appeared upon the water, a great way off, a certain thing that shone very brightly. And this drew near with great speed, and as it came nigh, behold! it was a boat all of carven brass. And the prow of the boat was carved into the form of a head of a beautiful woman, and upon either side were wings like the wings of a swan. And the boat moved upon the water like a swan—very swiftly—so that long lines, like to silver threads,

girdle: Here, waist.

92

stretched far away behind, across the face of the water, which otherwise was like unto glass for smoothness. And when the brazen boat had reached the bank it rested there and moved no more.

Then the Lady of the Lake bade King Arthur to enter the boat, and so he entered it. And immediately he had done so, the boat moved away from the bank as swiftly as it had come thither. And Merlin and the Lady of the Lake stood upon the margin of the water, and gazed after King Arthur and the brazen boat.

And King Arthur beheld that the boat floated swiftly across the lake to where was the arm uplifting the sword, and that the arm and the sword moved not but remained where they were.

Then King Arthur reached forth and took the sword in his hand, and immediately the arm disappeared beneath the water, and King Arthur held the sword and the scabbard thereof and the belt thereof in his hand and, lo! they were his own.

Then verily his heart swelled with joy an it would burst within his bosom, for Excalibur was an hundred times more beautiful than he had thought possible. Wherefore his heart was nigh breaking for pure joy at having obtained that magic sword.

Then the brazen boat bore him very quickly back to the land again and he stepped ashore where stood the Lady of the Lake and Merlin. And when he stood upon the shore, he gave the Lady great thanks beyond measure for all that she had done for to aid him in his great undertaking; and she gave him cheerful and pleasing words in reply.

Then King Arthur saluted the lady, as became him, and, having mounted his war-horse, and Merlin having mounted his palfrey, they rode away thence upon their business—the King's heart still greatly expanded with pure delight at having for his own that beautiful sword—the most beautiful and the most famous sword in all the world.

scabbard: A case or sheath to protect the blade of a sword.

sanctuary: A holy place or refuge.

Anon: In a little while.
noon-tide: Mid-day.

diligence: Careful attention.

That night King Arthur and Merlin abided with the holy hermit at the forest sanctuary, and when the next morning had come (the King having bathed himself in the ice-cold forest fountain, and being exceedingly refreshed thereby) they took their departure, offering thanks to that saintly man for the harborage he had given them.

Anon, about noon-tide, they reached the valley of the Sable Knight, and there were all things appointed exactly as when King Arthur had been there before: to wit, that gloomy castle, the lawn of smooth grass, the apple-tree covered over with shields, and the bridge whereon hung that single shield of sable.

"Now, Merlin," quoth King Arthur, "I do this time most strictly forbid thee for to interfere in this quarrel. Nor shalt thou, under pain of my displeasure, exert any of thy arts of magic in my behalf. So hearken thou to what I say, and heed it with all possible diligence."

Thereupon, straightway, the King rode forth upon the bridge and, seizing the brazen mall, he smote upon the sable shield with all his might and main. Immediately the portcullis of the castle was let fall as afore told, and, in the same manner as that other time, the Sable Knight rode forth therefrom, already bedight and equipped for the encounter. So he came to the bridge-head and there King Arthur spake to him in this wise: "Sir Pellinore, we do now know one another entirely well, and each doth judge that he hath cause of quarrel with the other: thou, that I, for mine own reasons as seemed to me to be fit, have taken away from thee thy kingly estate, and have driven thee into this forest solitude: I, that thou has set thyself up here for to do injury and affront to knights and lords and other people of this kingdom of mine. Wherefore, seeing that I am here as an errant Knight, I do challenge thee for to fight with me, man to man, until either thou or I have conquered the other."

Unto this speech King Pellinore bowed his head in obedience, and thereupon he wheeled his horse, and, riding

to some little distance, took his place where he had afore
stood. And King Arthur also rode to some little distance, and
took his station where he had afore stood. At the same time
there came forth from the castle one of those tall pages clad
all in sable, pied with crimson, and gave to King Arthur a
good, stout spear of ash-wood, well seasoned and untried in
battle; and when the two Knights were duly prepared, they
shouted and drave their horses together, the one smiting the
other so fairly in the midst of his defences that the spears
shivered in the hand of each, bursting all into small splinters
as they had aforetime done.

Then each of these two knights immediately voided his
horse with great skill and address, and drew each his sword.
And thereupon they fell to at a combat, so furious and so
violent, that two wild bulls upon the mountains could not
have engaged in a more desperate encounter.

address: Dexterity.

But now, having Excalibur for to aid him in his battle,
King Arthur soon overcame his enemy. For he gave him
several wounds and yet received none himself, nor did he
shed a single drop of blood in all that fight, though his
enemy's armor was in a little while all stained with crimson.
And at last King Arthur delivered so vehement a stroke that
King Pellinore was entirely benumbed thereby, wherefore his
sword and his shield fell down from their defence, his thighs
trembled beneath him and he sank unto his knees upon the
ground. Then he called upon King Arthur to have mercy,
saying, "Spare my life and I will yield myself unto thee."

And King Arthur said, "I will spare thee and I will do more
than that. For now that thou hast yielded thyself unto me,
lo! I will restore unto thee thy power and estate. For I bear
no ill-will toward thee, Pellinore, ne'theless, I can brook no
rebels against my power in this realm. For, as God judges me,
I do declare that I hold singly in my sight the good of the
people of my kingdom. Wherefore, he who is against me is
also against them, and he who is against them is also against
me. But now that thou hast acknowledged me I will take thee

into my favor. Only as a pledge of thy good faith toward me in the future, I shall require it of thee that thou shalt send me as hostage of thy good-will, thy two eldest sons, to wit: Sir Aglaval and Sir Lamorack. Thy young son, Dornar, thou mayest keep with thee for thy comfort."

So those two young knights above mentioned came to the Court of King Arthur, and they became very famous knights, and by and by were made fellows in great honor of the Round Table.

And King Arthur and King Pellinore went together into the castle of King Pellinore, and there King Pellinore's wounds were dressed and he was made comfortable. That night King Arthur abode in the castle of King Pellinore, and when the next morning had come, he and Merlin returned unto the Court of the King, where it awaited him in the forest at that place where he had established it.

Now King Arthur took very great pleasure unto himself as he and Merlin rode together in return through that forest; for it was the leafiest time of all the year, what time the woodlands decked themselves in their best apparel of clear, bright green. Each bosky dell and dingle was full of the perfume of the thickets, and in every tangled depth the small bird sang with all his might and main, and as though he would burst his little throat with the melody of his singing. And the ground beneath the horses' feet was so soft with fragrant moss that the ear could not hear any sound of hoof-beats upon the earth. And the bright yellow sunlight came down through the leaves so that all the ground was scattered over with a great multitude of trembling circles as of pure yellow gold. And, anon, that sunlight would fall down upon the armed knight as he rode, so that every little while his armor appeared to catch fire with a great glory, shining like a sudden bright star amid the dark shadows of the woodland.

bosky dell and dingle: Secluded wooded valley and glen.

96

So it was that King Arthur took great joy in that forest land, for he was without ache or pain of any sort and his heart was very greatly elated with the wonderfulness of the success of that adventure into which he had entered. For in that adventure he had not only won a very bitter enemy into a friend who should be of great usefulness and satisfaction to him, but likewise, he had obtained for himself a sword, the like of which the world had never before beheld. And whenever he would think of that singularly splendid sword which now hung by his side, and whenever he remembered that land of Faery into which he had wandered, and of that which had befallen him therein, his heart would become so greatly elated with pure joyousness that he hardly knew how to contain himself because of the great delight that filled his entire bosom.

elated: Overjoyed.

And, indeed, I know of no greater good that I could wish for you in all of your life than to have you enjoy such happiness as cometh to one when he hath done his best endeavor and hath succeeded with great entirety in his undertaking. For then all the world appears to be filled as with a bright shining light, and the body seemeth to become so elated that the feet are uplifted from heaviness and touch the earth very lightly because of the lightness of the spirit within. Wherefore, it is, that if I could have it in my power to give you the very best that the world hath to give, I would wish that you might win your battle as King Arthur won his battle at that time, and that you might ride homeward in such triumph and joyousness as filled him that day, and that the sunlight might shine around you as it shone around him, and that the breezes might blow and that all the little birds might sing with might and main as they sang for him, and that your heart also might sing its song of rejoicing in the pleasantness of the world in which you live.

Now as they rode thus through the forest together, Merlin said to the King: "Lord, which wouldst thou rather have, Excalibur, or the sheath that holds him?" To which King Arthur replied, "Ten thousand times would I rather have Excalibur than his sheath." "In that thou art wrong, my Lord," said Merlin, "for let me tell thee, that though Excalibur is of so great a temper that he may cut in twain either a feather or a bar of iron, yet is his sheath of such a sort that he who wears it can suffer no wound in battle, neither may he lose a single drop of blood. In witness whereof, thou mayst remember that, in thy late battle with King Pellinore, thou didst suffer no wound, neither didst thou lose any blood."

Then King Arthur directed a countenance of great displeasure upon his companion and he said, "Now, Merlin, I do declare that thou hast taken from me the entire glory of that battle which I have lately fought. For what credit may there be to any knight who fights his enemy by means of

cut in twain: Cut in two pieces.

enchantment such as thou tellest me of? And, indeed, I am minded to take this glorious sword back to that magic lake and to cast it therein where it belongeth; for I believe that a knight should fight by means of his own strength, and not by means of magic."

"My Lord," said Merlin, "assuredly thou art entirely right in what thou holdest. But thou must bear in mind that thou art not as an ordinary errant knight, but that thou art a King, and that thy life belongeth not unto thee, but unto thy people. Accordingly thou hast no right to imperil it, but shouldst do all that lieth in thy power for to preserve it. Wherefore thou shouldst keep that sword so that it may safeguard thy life."

imperil: Endanger.

Then King Arthur meditated that saying for a long while in silence; and when he spake it was in this wise: "Merlin, thou art right in what thou sayest, and, for the sake of my people, I will keep both Excalibur for to fight for them, and likewise his sheath for to preserve my life for their sake. Ne'theless, I will never use him again saving in serious battle." And King Arthur held to that saying, so that thereafter he did no battle in sport excepting with lance and a-horseback.

King Arthur kept Excalibur as the chiefest treasure of all his possessions. For he said to himself, "Such a sword as this is fit for a king above other kings and a lord above other lords. Now, as God hath seen fit for to intrust that sword into my keeping in so marvellous a manner as fell about, so must He mean that I am to be His servant for to do unusual things. Wherefore I will treasure this noble weapon not more for its excellent worth than because it shall be unto me as a sign of those great things that God, in His mercy, hath evidently ordained for me to perform for to do Him service."

So King Arthur had made for Excalibur a strong chest or coffer, bound around with many bands of wrought iron, studded all over with great nails of iron, and locked with three great padlocks. In this strong-box he kept Excalibur lying upon a cushion of crimson silk and wrapped in swathings of fine linen, and very few people ever beheld the sword in its glory excepting when it shone like a sudden flame in the uproar of battle.

swathings: Bandings.

For when the time came for King Arthur to defend his realm or his subjects from their enemies, then he would take out the sword, and fasten it upon the side of his body; and when he did so he was like unto a hero of God girt with a blade of shining lightning. Yea; at such times Excalibur shone with so terrible a brightness that the very sight thereof would shake the spirits of every wrong-doer with such great fear that he would, in a manner, suffer the pangs of death ere ever the edge of the blade had touched his flesh.

pangs: Pains.

So King Arthur treasured Excalibur and the sword remained with him for all of his life, wherefore the name of Arthur and of Excalibur are one. So, I believe that that sword is the most famous of any that ever was seen or heard tell of in all the Courts of Chivalry.

As for the sheath of the blade, King Arthur lost that through the treachery of one who should, by rights, have been his dearest friend (as you shall hear of anon), and in the end the loss of that miraculous sheath brought it about that he suffered a very great deal of pain and sorrow.

treachery: Betrayal, deception.

All that also you shall read of, God willing, in due season.

So endeth the story of the winning of Excalibur, and may God give unto you in your life, that you may have His truth to aid you, like a shining sword, for to overcome your enemies; and may He give you Faith (for Faith containeth Truth as a scabbard containeth its sword), and may that Faith heal all your wounds of sorrow as the sheath of Excalibur healed all the wounds of him who wore that excellent weapon. For with Truth and Faith girded upon you, you shall be as well able to fight all your battles as did that noble hero of old, whom men called King Arthur.

girded upon: Put around.

Part Three
The Winning of a Queen

So, having told you how King Arthur obtained that very excellent sword, Excalibur, for a weapon of defence, I shall now presently recount sundry other noble and knightly adventures whereby he won for himself a most beautiful and gentle lady for his Queen.

For, though all the world is very well acquainted with the renown of that perfectly gracious dame, the Lady Guinevere, yet I do not think that the whole story of those adventures by the which King Arthur won her good favor hath ever yet been told.

So as the matter hereinafter to be related contains not only the narrative of that affair, but also the account of a certain enchanted disguise which King Arthur assumed for his purposes, as well as sundry adventures of very knightly daring which he undertook, I have great hope that he who reads what I have written shall find it both an agreeable and an entertaining history.

hereinafter: After this.

Now, upon a certain day King Arthur proclaimed a high feast, which was held at Carleon upon Usk. Many noble guests were bidden, and an exceedingly splendid Court gathered at the King's castle. For at that feast there sat seven kings and five queens in royal state, and there were high lords and beautiful ladies of degree, to the number of three score and seven; and there were a multitude of those famous knights of the King's Court who were reckoned the most renowned in arms in all of Christendom. And of all this great gathering of kings, lords, and knights, not one man looked askance at his neighbor, but all were united in good fellowship. Wherefore, when the young King looked about him and beheld such peace and amity among all these noble lords where, aforetime, had been discord and ill-regard: "Certes," quoth he to himself, "it is wonderful how this reign of mine hath knit men together in kindness and good fellowship!" And because of such thoughts as these, his spirit took wings like unto a bird and sang within him.

Now while the King sat thus at feast, lo! there came an herald-messenger from the west-country. And the herald came and stood before the King, and said: "Greeting to thee, King Arthur!"

Then the King said: "Speak, and tell me, what is thy message?"

To which the herald made reply: "I come from King

1

HOW KING ARTHUR WENT TO TINTAGALON WITH FOUR OF HIS COURT, AND HOW HE DISGUISED HIMSELF FOR A CERTAIN PURPOSE.

Carleon: One of the three towns with which Arthur is associated.

askance: Suspiciously.

amity: Friendship, good will.

Leodegrance of Cameliard, who is in sore trouble. For thus it is: His enemy and thine enemy, King Ryence of North Wales (he who at one time in contempt of thee commanded thee to send him thy beard for to trim his mantle), doth make sundry demands of my master, King Leodegrance, which demands King Leodegrance is altogether loath to fulfil. And King Ryence of North Wales threateneth to bring war into Cameliard because King Leodegrance doth not immediately fulfil those demands. Now King Leodegrance hath no such array of knights and armed men as he one time had gathered about him for to defend his kingdom against assault. For, since thou in thy majesty hath brought peace to this realm and hath reduced the power of all those kings under thee, those knights who once made the Court of King Leodegrance so famous have gone elsewhither for to seek better opportunities for their great valor and prowess at arms than his peaceful Court may afford. Wherefore my master, King Leodegrance, doth beseech aid of thee, who art his King and Overlord."

To these things that the herald-messenger said, King Arthur, and all that Court that feasted with him, listened in entire silence. And the King's countenance, which erstwhiles had been expanded with cheerfulness, became overcast and dark with anger. "Ha!" he cried, "this is, verily, no good news that thou hast brought hither to our feast. Now I will give what aid I am able to thy master, King Leodegrance, in this extremity, and that right speedily. But tell me, sir herald, what things are they that King Ryence demandeth of thy master?"

"That I will tell you, Lord," quoth the herald-messenger. "Firstly, King Ryence maketh demand upon my master of a great part of those lands of Cameliard that march upon the borders of North Wales. Secondly, he maketh demand that the Lady Guinevere, the King's daughter, be delivered in marriage unto Duke Mordaunt of North Umber, who is of kin unto King Ryence, and that Duke, though a mighty warrior, is so evil of appearance, and so violent of temper, that I believe that there is not his like for ugliness or for madness of humor in all of the world."

Now when King Arthur heard this that the messenger said he was immediately seized with an extraordinary passion of anger. For his eyes appeared, an it were, to shoot forth sparks of pure light, his face flamed like fire, and he ground his teeth together like the stones of a quern. Then he immediately rose from the chair where he sat and went forth from that place, and all those who beheld his anger shuddered thereat and turned their eyes away from his countenance.

Then King Arthur went into an inner room of the castle by himself, and there he walked up and down for a great while, and in that time no one of his household dared to come nigh to him. And the reason of the King's wrath was this: that ever since he had lain wounded and sick nigh unto death in the forest, he bare in mind how the Lady Guinevere had suddenly appeared before him like some tall, straight, shining angel who had descended unto him out of Paradise—all full of pity, and exceedingly beautiful. Wherefore, at thought of that wicked, mad Duke Mordaunt of North Umber making demand unto marriage with her, he was seized with a rage so violent that it shook his spirit like a mighty wind.

So, for a long while, he walked up and down in his wrath as aforesaid, and no one durst come nigh unto him, but all stood afar off, watching him from a distance.

Then, after a while, he gave command that Merlin, and Sir Ulfius, and Sir Kay should come to him at that place where he was. And when they had come thither he talked to them for a considerable time, bidding Merlin for to make ready to go upon a journey with him, and bidding Sir Ulfius and Sir Kay for to gather together a large army of chosen knights and armed men, and to bring that army straightway into those

quern: A small hand-mill consisting of two circular stones for grinding pepper, corn, etc.

parts coadjacent to the royal castle of Tintagalon, which same standeth close to the borders of North Wales and of Cameliard.

So Sir Ulfius and Sir Kay went about to do as King Arthur commanded, and Merlin also went about to do as he commanded; and the next day King Arthur and Merlin, together with certain famous knights of the King's Court who were the most approved at arms of all those about him—to wit, Sir Gawaine, and Sir Ewaine (who were nephews unto the King), and Sir Pellias and Sir Geraint, the son of Erbin—set forth for Tintagalon across the forest-land of Usk.

So they travelled for all that day and a part of the next, and that without adventure or misadventure of any sort. So they came, at last, to that large and noble castle, hight Tintagalon, which guards the country bordering upon Cameliard and North Wales. Here King Arthur was received with great rejoicing; for whithersoever the King went the people loved him very dearly. Wherefore the folk of Tintagalon were very glad when he came unto them.

Now the morning after King Arthur had come unto Tintagalon (the summer night having been very warm), he and Merlin were glad to arise betimes to go abroad for to enjoy the dewy freshness of the early daytime. So, in the cool of the day, they walked together in the garden (which was a very pleasant place), and beneath the shadow of a tall, straight tower. And all around about were many trees with a good shade, where the little birds sang sweetly in the cheerfulness of the summer weather.

And here King Arthur opened his mind very freely to Merlin, and he said: "Merlin, I do believe that the Lady Guinevere is the fairest lady in all of the world; wherefore my heart seems ever to be entirely filled with love for her, and that to such a degree that I think of her continually by day (whether I be eating, or drinking, or walking, or sitting still,

betimes: Early in the morning.

106

or going about my business), and likewise I dream of her many times at night. And this has been the case with me, Merlin, ever since a month ago, when I lay sick in that hermit's cell in the forest, what time she came and stood beside me like a shining angel out of Paradise. So I am not willing that any other man than I should have her for his wife.

"Now I know very well that thou art wonderfully cunning in those arts of magic that may change a man in his appearance so that even those who know him best may not recognize him. Wherefore I very greatly desire it of thee that thou wilt so disguise me that I may go, unknown of any man, into Cameliard, and that I may dwell there in such a way that I may see the Lady Guinevere every day. For I tell thee very truly that I greatly desire to behold her in such a wise that she may not be in any way witting of my regard. Likewise I would fain see for myself how great may be the perils that encompass King Leodegrance—the King being my right good friend."

"My Lord King," said Merlin, "it shall be as thou desirest, and this morning I will cause thee to be so disguised that no one in all the world shall be able to know thee who thou art."

So that morning, a little before the prime, Merlin came unto the King where he was and gave him a little cap. And the cap was of such a sort that when the King set it upon his head he assumed, upon the instant, the appearance of a rude and rustic fellow from the country-side. Then the King commanded that a jerkin of rough frieze should be brought to him, and with this he covered his royal and knightly vestments, and with it he hid that golden collar and its jewel pendent, which he continually wore about his neck. Then, setting the cap upon his head, he assumed at once the guise of that peasant hind.

Whereupon, being thus entirely disguised, he quitted

jerkin of rough frieze: A close-fitting jacket of coarse wool.

Tintagalon unknown of any man, and took his way a-foot unto the town of Cameliard.

Now toward the slanting of the day he drew nigh to that place, and lo! he beheld before him a large and considerable town of many comely houses with red walls and shining windows. And the houses of the town sat all upon a high, steep hill, the one overlooking the other, and the town itself was encompassed around about by a great wall, high and strong. And a great castle guarded the town, and the castle had very many towers and roofs. And all round about the tower were many fair gardens and lawns and meadows, and several orchards and groves of trees with thick and pleasing shade. Now at that time of the day the sky behind the tower was all, as it were, an entire flame of fire, so that the towers and the battlements of the castle and the roofs and the chimneys thereof stood altogether black against the brightness of the light. And, behold! great flocks of pigeons encircled the towers of the castle in a continual flight against that fiery sky. So, because King Arthur was a-weary with walking for all that day, it appeared to him that he had hardly ever beheld in all of his life so fair and pleasing a place as that excellent castle with its gardens and lawns and groves of trees.

Thus came King Arthur unto the castle of Cameliard, in the guise of a poor peasant from the country-side, and no man in all of the world knew him who he was.

So, having reached the castle, he made inquiries for the head gardener thereof; and when he had speech with the gardener he besought him that he might be taken into service into that part of the garden that appertained to the dwelling-place of the Lady Guinevere. Then the gardener looked upon him and saw that he was tall and strong and well framed, wherefore he liked him very well and took him into service even as he desired.

And thus it was that King Arthur of Britain became a gardener's boy at Cameliard.

Now the King was very glad to be in that garden; for in
this pleasant summer season the Lady Guinevere came every
day to walk with her damsels among the flowers, and King
Arthur, all disguised as a peasant gardener boy, beheld her
very many times when she came thither.

So King Arthur abode at that place for above a week, and
he took no care that in all that time he enjoyed none of his
kingly estate, but was only gardener's boy in the castle
garden of Cameliard.

ante-room: A room before or forming an entrance to another.
casement: A hinged frame forming a window.

ewer: A tall, slender vessel of rich material and highly decorative.

bosom: Upper chest.

Now it happened upon a day when the weather was very warm, that one of the damsels who was in attendance upon the Lady Guinevere, arose all in the early morning whiles the air was still cool and refreshing. So, leaving the Lady Guinevere still sleeping, this damsel, whose name was Mellicene of the White Hand, went into the ante-room and, opening the casement thereof, looked forth into that garden of roses which adjoined the Lady Guinevere's bower.

Now there was at that place a carven marble figure of a youth, holding in his arms a marble ewer, and a fountain of water, as clear as crystal, flowed out from the ewer into a basin of marble. And the figure, and the fountain, and the marble basin into which the fountain flowed lay beneath the shadow of a linden-tree. And all around was a thick growth of roses, so that the place was entirely hidden, saving only from those windows of the castle that were above.

So it befell that as the damsel looked down thitherward out of the window, she beheld a very wonderful sight. For, lo! a strange knight kneeled beside the fountain and bathed his face and his bosom in the crystal water thereof. And the damsel saw that the sunlight fell down through the leaves of the linden-tree and lay upon that strange knight. And she perceived that his hair and his beard were of the color of red gold—shining surpassingly in the brightness of the morning. And she beheld that his brow and his throat and his bosom were white like alabaster. And she beheld that around his neck and shoulders there hung a golden collar of marvellous beauty, so that when the sunlight shone upon it it flashed like pure lightning.

So, beholding this strange appearance—as it were a vision—the damsel Mellicine stood for a long while, all entranced with wonder and with pleasure, and wist not whether that which she saw was a dream or no dream, nor whether he who sat there was a spirit, or whether he was a man of flesh and blood.

Then, by and by, recovering somewhat from her astonishment, she withdrew herself softly from the casement, and, turning about, ran fleetly down the turret stairs, and so came out thence into that fair and blooming garden at the foot of the tower. So she ran through the garden with all speed and silence, and thus came down an alley-way and to the marble fountain and the linden-trees and the rose-trees around about where she had anon beheld that strange knight bathing himself in the crystal waters.

But King Arthur had heard the coming of that damsel, and had speedily set the cap upon his head again. So that when the damsel Mellicene came thither, she found no one by the fountain but the gardener's boy. Of him she demanded: "Who art thou, fellow? And why sittest thou here by the fountain?"

And unto her he replied: "I am the gardener's lad who came a short time ago to take service at this place."

"Then tell me, fellow," quoth she, "and tell me truly. Who was that young knight who was here beside the fountain but now, and whither hath he gone?" "Lady, whereunto," he said, "there has been no one at this fountain this day, but only I."

"Nay, fellow," she cried, "thou art deceiving me, for I do assure thee that with mine own eyes I beheld but now, where a strange young knight sat bathing himself in the waters of this fountain." And the gardener's boy said, "Lady, that which I have told you is the very truth, for indeed there hath no one been here this morn but only I. Wherefore, an thou deemest thou hast seen anyone else, thou art certainly mistaken."

an thou deemest: If you think.

At this the damsel set her look upon him, in great perplexity. Likewise, she marvelled very greatly, for she could not altogether disbelieve him. Nor yet could she entirely believe him either, because her eyes had beheld that which she had beheld, and she wotted that she had not been mistaken. Therefore she knew not what to think, and, because of her perplexity, she felt a very great displeasure at that gardener's boy. "Truly, wherefore," she said, "if thou art deceiving me, I shall certainly cause thee to suffer a great deal of pain, for I shall have thee whipped with cords." Thereupon she turned and went away from that place, much marvelling at that strange thing, and wondering what it all signified.

That morning she told unto the Lady Guinevere all that she had seen, but the Lady Guinevere only laughed at her and mocked her, telling her that she had been asleep and dreaming, when she beheld that vision. And, indeed, the damsel herself had begun to think this must be the case. Nevertheless, she thereafter looked out every morning from her casement window, albeit she beheld nothing for a great while, for King Arthur came not soon to that place again.

So, by and by, there befell another certain morning when she looked out of the casement and, lo! there sat that strange knight by the fountain once more as he had aforetime sat. And he bathed his face and his bosom in the water as he had aforetime done. And he appeared as comely and as noble as he had appeared before; and his hair and his young beard shone like gold as they had shone before in the sun. And this time she beheld that his collar of gold lay upon the brink of the fountain beside him, and it sparkled with great splendor in the sunlight the whiles he bathed his bosom. Then, after that damsel had regarded him for a considerable time, she ran with all speed to the chamber where the Lady Guinevere still lay, and she cried in a loud voice, "Lady! lady! arouse thee and come with me! For, lo! that same young knight whom I beheld before, is even now bathing himself at the fountain under the linden-tree."

Then the Lady Guinevere, greatly marvelling, aroused herself right quickly, and, dighting herself with all speed, went with the damsel unto that casement window which looked out into that part of the garden.

And there she herself beheld the young knight where he laved himself at the fountain. And she saw that his hair and

albeit: (all BE it) Even though.

112

his beard shone like gold in the sunlight; and she saw that his undervestment was of purple linen threaded with gold; and she saw that beside him lay that cunningly wrought collar of gold inset with many jewels of various colors, and the collar shone with great splendor where it lay upon the marble verge of the fountain.

verge: The edge, rim.

Somewhiles she gazed, exceedingly astonished; then she commanded the damsel Mellicene for to come with her, and therewith she turned and descended the turret stairs, and went quickly out into the garden, as her damsel had done aforetime. Then, as that damsel had done, she straightway hastened with all speed down the alley-way toward the fountain.

But, behold! when she had come there, she found no young knight, but only the gardener boy, exactly as had happened with the damsel Mellicene aforetime. For King Arthur had heard her coming, and had immediately put that enchanted cap upon his head. Then the Lady Guinevere marvelled very greatly to find there only the gardener's boy, and she wist not what to think of so strange a thing. Wherefore she demanded of him, even as Mellicene had done, whither had gone the young knight whom she had beheld anon there at the fountain. And unto her the gardener lad made answer as aforetime: "Lady! there hath been no one at this place at any time this morning, but only I."

Now when King Arthur had donned his cap at the coming of the Lady, he had, in his great haste, forgotten his golden collar, and this Guinevere beheld where it lay shining very brightly, beside the margin of the fountain. "How now!" quoth she. "Wouldst thou dare to make a mock of me? Now tell me, thou fellow, do gardeners' boys in the land whence thou didst come wear golden collars about their necks like unto that collar that lieth yonder beside the fountain? Now, an I had thee well whipped, it would be thy rightful due. But take thou that bauble yonder and give it unto him to whom it doth rightfully belong, and tell him from me that it doth ill

bauble: A trinket.

113

become a true belted knight for to hide himself away in the privy gardens of a lady." Then turned she with the damsel Mellicene, and left she that place and went back again into her bower.

Yet, indeed for all that day, as she sat over her 'broidery, she did never cease to marvel and to wonder how it was possible that that strange young knight should so suddenly have vanished away and left only the poor gardener's boy in his stead. Nor, for a long time, might she unriddle that strange thing.

Then, of a sudden, at that time when the heat of the day was sloping toward the cooler part of the afternoon, she aroused herself because of a thought that had come in an instant unto her. So she called the damsel Mellicene to come to her, and she bade her to go and tell the gardener's lad for to fetch her straightway a basket of fresh roses for to adorn her tower chamber.

So Mellicene went and did as she bade, and after considerable time the gardener's lad came bearing a great basket of roses. And, lo! he wore his cap upon his head. And all the damsels in waiting upon the Lady Guinevere, when they saw how he wore his cap in her presence, cried out upon him, and Mellicene of the White Hand demanded of him: "What! How now, Sir boor! Dost thou know so little of what is due unto a king's daughter that thou dost wear thy cap even in the presence of the Lady Guinevere? Now I bid thee straightway to take thy cap off thy head."

And to her King Arthur made answer: "Lady, I cannot take off my cap."

Quoth the Lady Guinevere: "And why canst thou not take off thy cap, thou surly fellow?"

surly: Rude.

"Lady," said he, "I cannot take off my cap, because I have an ugly place upon my head."

"Then wear thy cap," quoth the Lady Guinevere. "Only fetch thou the roses unto me."

114

And so at her bidding, he brought the roses to her. But when he had come nigh unto the lady, she, of a sudden, snatched at the cap and plucked it off from his head. Then, lo! he was upon the instant transformed; for instead of the gardener's boy there stood before the Lady Guinevere and her damsel the appearance of a noble young knight with hair and beard like threads of gold. Then he let fall his basket of roses so that the flowers were scattered all over the floor, and he stood and looked at all who were there. And some of those damsels in attendance upon the Lady Guinevere shrieked, and others stood still from pure amazement and wist not how to believe what their eyes beheld. But not one of those ladies knew that he whom she beheld was King Arthur. Nevertheless the Lady Guinevere remembered that this was the knight whom she had found so sorely wounded, lying in the hermit's cell in the forest.

Then she laughed and flung him back his cap again. "Take thy cap," quoth she, "and go thy ways, thou gardener's boy who hath an ugly place upon his head." Thus she said because she was minded to mock him.

But King Arthur did not reply to her, but straightway, with great sobriety of aspect, set his cap upon his head again. So resuming his humble guise once more, he turned and quitted that place, leaving those roses scattered all over the floor even as they had fallen.

sobriety of aspect: Seriousness of expression.

And after that time, whenever the Lady Guinevere would come upon the gardener's lad in the garden, she would say unto her damsel in such a voice that he might hear her speech: "Lo! yonder is the gardener's lad who hath an ugly place upon his head so that he must always wear his cap for to hide it."

Thus she spake openly, mocking at him; but privily she bade her damsels to say naught concerning these things, but to keep unto themselves all those things which had befallen.

Now, upon a certain day at this time there came a messenger to the Court of King Leodegrance, with news that King Ryence of North Wales and Duke Mordaunt of North Umber were coming thither and that they brought with them a very noble and considerable Court of knights and lords. At this news King Leodegrance was much troubled in spirit, for he wist not what such a visit might betoken; and yet he greatly feared that it boded ill for him. So on that day when King Ryence and the Duke of North Umber appeared before the castle, King Leodegrance went forth to greet them and they three met together in the meadows that lie beneath the castle walls of Cameliard.

There King Leodegrance bade those others welcome in such manner as was fitting, desiring them that they should come into the castle with him so that he might entertain them according to their degree.

But to this courtesy upon the part of King Leodegrance, King Ryence deigned no pleasing reply. "Nay," quoth he, "we go not with thee into thy castle, King Leodegrance, until we learn whether thou art our friend or our enemy. For just

2

HOW KING RYENCE CAME TO CAMELIARD AND HOW KING ARTHUR FOUGHT WITH THE DUKE OF NORTH UMBER.

now we are, certes, no such good friends with thee that we care to sit down at thy table and eat of thy salt. Nor may we be aught but enemies of thine until thou hast first satisfied our demands; to wit, that thou givest to me those lands which I demand of thee and that thou givest unto my cousin, Duke Mordaunt of North Umber, the Lady Guinevere to be his wife. In these matters thou hast it in thy power to make us either thy friends or thine enemies. Wherefore we shall abide here, outside of thy castle, for five days, in the which time thou mayst frame thine answer, and so we may know whether we shall be friends or enemies."

"And in the meantime," quoth Duke Mordaunt of North Umber, "I do hold myself ready for to contest my right unto the hand of the Lady Guinevere with any knight of thy Court who hath a mind to deny my just title thereto; and if thou hast no knight in all thy Court who can successfully assay a bout of arms with me, thou thyself canst hardly hope to succeed in defending thyself against that great army of knights whom King Ryence hath gathered together to bring against thee in case thou denyest us that which we ask."

Then was King Leodegrance exceedingly cast down in his spirits, for he feared those proud lords and he wist not what to say in answer to them. Wherefore he turned and walked back into his castle again, beset with great anxiety and sorrow of spirit. And King Ryence, and Duke Mordaunt and their Court of lords and knights pitched their pavilions in those meadows over against the castle, so that the plain was entirely covered with those pavilions. And there they took up their inn with great rejoicing and with the sound of feasting and singing and merry-making, for it was an exceeding noble Court King Ryence had gathered about him.

And when the next morning had come Duke Mordaunt of North Umber went forth clad all in armor of proof. And he rode up and down the field before the castle and gave great challenge to those within; daring any knight to come forth

beset: Set upon, filled with.

for to meet him in knightly encounter. "Ho!" he cried, "how now, ye Knights of Cameliard! Is there no one to come forth to meet me? How then may ye hope to contend with the Knights of North Wales, an ye fear to meet with one single Knight from North Umber?" So he scoffed at them in his pride, and none dared to come forth from Cameliard against him. For the Duke of North Umber was one of the most famous knights of his day, and one of exceeding strength and success at arms, and there was now, in these times of peace, no one of King Leodegrance's Court who was at all able to face a warrior of his approved skill and valor. Wherefore, no one took up that challenge which the Duke of North Umber gave to the Court of Cameliard. Meantime many people gathered upon the walls of Cameliard and gazed down therefrom upon that proud and haughty duke, all bedight in his splendid armor, and all were grieved and ashamed that there was no one in that peaceful town to go out against him. And all the lords and knights of King Ryence's Court came and stood in front of the King's pavilion and laughed and clapped their hands together, and cheered Duke Mordaunt, as he so rode up and down before them. And the greater they were expanded with mirth, the more abashed were the people of Cameliard. "Ho! Ho!" cried that proud Duke. "How now! Will no one come forth to meet me? How then may ye of Cameliard hope to face the King of North Wales and all his knightly array of which I am but one man?" And the people of Cameliard, gathered upon the walls, listened to him with shame and sorrow.

Now all this while King Arthur digged in the garden; but nevertheless, he was well aware of everything that passed and of how that the Duke of North Umber rode up and down so proudly before the castle walls. So, of a sudden, it came to him that he could not abide this any longer. Wherefore he laid aside his spade and went out secretly by a postern way, and so up into the town.

postern: Private.

119

Now there was in Cameliard an exceedingly rich merchant, by name Ralph of Cardiff, and the renown of his possessions and his high estate had reached even unto King Arthur's ears at Carleon. Accordingly it was unto his house that King Arthur directed his steps.

And while he was in a narrow way, not far from the merchant's house, he took off his magic cap of disguise and assumed somewhat of his noble appearance once more, for he was now of a mind to show his knightliness unto those who looked upon him. Accordingly, when he stood before the rich merchant in his closet, and when the merchant looked up into his face, he wist not what to think to behold so noble a lord clad all in frieze. For though King Arthur was a stranger to the good man, so that he knew not his countenance, yet that merchant wist that he was no ordinary knight, but that he must assuredly be one of high degree and in authority, even though he was clad in frieze.

Then King Arthur opened the breast of his jerkin and showed the merchant the gold collar that hung around his neck. And also he showed beneath the rough coat of frieze how that there was an undergarment of fine purple silk embroidered with gold. And then he showed to the good man his own signet ring, and when the merchant saw it, he knew it to be the ring of the King of Britain. Wherefore, beholding these tokens of high and lordly authority, the merchant arose and stood before the King and doffed his cap.

"Sir Merchant," quoth the King, "know that I am a stranger knight in disguise in this place. Ne'theless, I may tell thee that I am a very good friend to King Leodegrance and wish him exceeding well. Thou art surely aware of how the Duke of North Umber rides continually up and down before the King's castle, and challenges anyone within to come forth for to fight against him in behalf of the Lady Guinevere. Now I am of a mind to assay that combat mine own self, and I hope a very great deal that I shall succeed in upholding the honor of Cameliard and of bringing shame upon its enemies.

"Sir Merchant, I know very well that thou hast several
suits of noble armor in thy treasury, for the fame of them
hath reached unto mine ears though I dwell a considerable
distance from this place. Wherefore I desire that thou shalt
provide me in the best manner that thou art able to do, so
that I may straightway assay a bout of arms with that Duke
of North Umber. Moreover, I do pledge thee my knightly
word that thou shalt be fully recompensed for the best suit
of armor that thou canst let me have, and that in a very little
while."

behests: Commands.

tepid: Lukewarm.

grateful to the person: Pleasing or agreeable to the body.

sarsanet: A very fine, soft silk.

juppon: A jacket worn with armor.

"My Lord," said Master Ralph, "I perceive that thou art no ordinary errant knight, but rather someone of extraordinary estate; wherefore it is a very great pleasure to fulfil all thy behests. But even an thou wert other than thou art, I would be altogether willing to equip thee with armor, seeing that thou hast a mind to ride forth against yonder duke."

Upon this he rang a little silver bell that stood nigh to him, and in answer to its sound several attendants immediately appeared. Into their hands he intrusted the person of the King, bidding them to do him extraordinary honor. Accordingly, certain of those attendants prepared for the King a bath of tepid water perfumed with ambergris, very grateful to the person. And after he was bathed in this bath and was wiped with soft linen towels, other attendants conducted him to a hall all hung with tapestries and 'broideries, and at this place a noble feast had been spread ready for his refreshment. Here that lordly merchant himself ministered to the King's wants, serving him with various meats—very dainty, and of several sorts—and likewise with fine white bread. And he poured him wine of various countries—some as red as ruby, others as yellow as gold; and indeed the King had hardly ever enjoyed a better feast than that which the merchant, Ralph of Cardiff, had thus spread for him.

And after he had entirely refreshed himself with eating, there came six pages richly clad in sarsanet of azure, and these, taking the King to an apartment of great state, they there clad him in a suit of Spanish armor, very cunningly wrought and all inlaid with gold. And the like of that armor was hardly to be found in all of the land. The juppon and the several trappings of the armor were all of satin and as white as milk. And the shield was white, and altogether without emblazonment or device of any sort. Then these attendants conducted the King into the courtyard, and there stood a noble war-horse, as white as milk, and all the trappings of the horse were of milk-white cloth without emblazonment or adornment of any sort; and the bridle and the bridle rein were all studded over with bosses of silver.

Then after the attendants had aided King Arthur to mount this steed, the lordly merchant came forward and gave him many words of good cheer, and so the king bade him adieu and rode away, all shining in white and glittering in fine armor, wherefore he resembled the full moon in harvest season.

And as he drave down the stony streets of the town, the people turned and gazed after him, for he made a very noble appearance as he passed along the narrow way between the houses of the town.

So King Arthur directed his way to the postern gate of the castle, and, having reached that place, he dismounted and tied his horse. Then he straightway entered the garden, and there, finding an attendant, he made demand that he should have present speech with the Lady Guinevere. So the attendant, all amazed at his lordly presence, went and delivered the message, and by and by the Lady Guinevere came, much wondering, and passed along a gallery with several of her damsels, until she had come over above where King Arthur was. And when King Arthur looked up and saw her above him, he loved her exceeding well. And he said to her: "Lady, I have great will to do thee such honor as I am able. For I go forth now to do combat with that Duke of North Umber who rides up and down before this castle. Moreover, I hope and verily believe that I shall encompass his downfall; accordingly, I do beseech of thee some token, such as a lady may give unto a knight for to wear when that knight rides forth to do her honor."

Then the Lady Guinevere said: "Certes, Sir Knight, I would that I knew who thou art. Yet, though I know not, nevertheless I am altogether willing for to take thee for my champion as thou offerest. So, touching that token thou

adieu: Farewell, goodbye.

speakest of, if thou wilt tell me what thing it is that thou desirest, I will gladly give it to thee."

"An that be so, Lady," said King Arthur, "I would fain have that necklace that thou wearest about thy throat. For, meseems that if I had that tied about my arm, I would find my valor greatly increased thereby."

"Pardee, Sir Knight," said the Lady, "what thou desirest of me thou shalt assuredly have." Thereupon speaking, she took from her long, smooth neck the necklace of pearls which she wore, and dropped the same down to King Arthur where he stood.

And King Arthur took the necklace and tied it about his arm, and he gave great thanks for it. Then he saluted the Lady Guinevere with very knightly grace, and she saluted him, and then, straightway, he went forth from that place, greatly expanded with joy that the Lady Guinevere had shown him such favor.

Now the report had gone about Cameliard that a knight was to go forth to fight the Duke of North Umber. Wherefore great crowds gathered upon the walls, and King Leodegrance and the Lady Guinevere and all the Court of the King came to that part of the castle walls overlooking the meadow where the Duke of North Umber defended. Wherefore, so great a concourse was presently assembled, that any knight might be encouraged to do his utmost before such a multitude as that which looked down upon the field.

Then of a sudden the portcullis of the castle was lifted, and the bridge let fall, and the White Champion rode forth to that encounter which he had undertaken. And, as he drave across that narrow bridge, the hoofs of his war-horse smote the boards with a noise like to thunder, and when he came out into the sunlight, lo! his armor flamed of a sudden like unto lightning and when the people saw him they shouted aloud.

Then when the Duke of North Umber beheld a knight all

clad in white, he rode straightway to him and spoke to him with words of knightly greeting. "Messire," he said, "I perceive that thou bearest no crest upon thy helm, nor hast thou a device of any sort upon thy shield, wherefore I know not who thou art. Ne'theless, I do believe that thou art a knight of good quality and of approved courage, or else thou wouldst not have thus come to this place."

"Certes, Sir Knight," said King Arthur, "I am of a quality equal to thine own. And as for my courage, I do believe that it hath been approved in as many encounters as even thine own hath been."

"Sir Knight," quoth the Duke of Umber, "thou speakest with a very large spirit. Ne'theless, thou mayst make such prayers as thou art able, for I shall now presently so cast thee down from thy seat, so that thou shalt never rise again; for so have I served better men than ever thou mayst hope to be."

To this King Arthur made answer with great calmness of demeanor: "That shall be according to the will of Heaven, Sir Knight, and not according to thy will."

So each knight saluted the other and rode to his assigned station, and there each dressed his spear and his shield, and made him ready for the encounter. Then a silence fell upon all so great that a man might hear his own heart beat in the stillness. So, for a small space, each knight sat like a statue made of iron. Then, of a sudden, each shouted to his war-horse, and drave spurs into his flank, and launched forth from his station. And so they met in the midst of the course with a noise like unto a violent thunder-clap. And lo! the spear of the Duke of North Umber burst into splinters unto the very truncheon thereof; but the spear of King Arthur broke not, but held, so that the Duke was cast out of his saddle like a windmill—whirling in the air and smiting the earth so that the ground shuddered beneath him. And indeed he rolled full three times over and over ere he ceased to fall.

Then all the people upon the wall shouted with might and

THE WINNING OF A QUEEN

crest....helm: A family coat of arms or seal commonly inscribed on a knight's shield and helmet.

seat: Here, saddle.

main, so that the noise thereof was altogether astonishing; for they had hardly hoped that their champion should have proved so extraordinarily strong and skilful.

Meanwhile, those of King Ryence's Court ran immediately to the Duke of Umber where he lay upon the earth, and they straightway unlaced his helm for to give him air. And first they thought that he was dead, and then they thought that he was like to die; for, behold! he lay without any life or motion. Nor did he recover from that swoon wherein he lay for the space of full two hours and more.

Now whilst the attendants were thus busied about Duke Mordaunt of North Umber, King Arthur sat his horse, very quietly, observing all that they did. Then, perceiving that his enemy was not dead, he turned him about and rode away from that place.

Nor did he return unto Cameliard at that time, for he deemed that he had not yet entirely done with these enemies to the peace of his realm, wherefore he was minded not yet to return the horse and the armor to the merchant, but to keep them for a while for another occasion.

So he bethought him of how, coming to Cameliard, he had passed through an arm of the forest where certain wood-choppers were at work felling the trees. Wherefore, remembering that place, he thought that he would betake him thither and leave his horse and armor in the care of those rude folk until he would need those things once more. So now he rode away into the country-side, leaving behind him the town and the castle and all the noise of shouting and rejoicing; nor did he once so much as turn his head to look back toward that place where he had so violently overthrown his enemy.

And now you shall presently hear of certain pleasant adventures of a very joyous sort that befell him ere he had accomplished all his purposes. For when a man is a king among men, as was King Arthur, then is he of such a calm and equal temper that neither victory nor defeat may cause him to become either unduly exalted in his own opinion or so troubled in spirit as to be altogether cast down into despair. So if you would become like to King Arthur, then you shall take all your triumphs as he took this victory, for you will not be turned aside from your final purposes by the great applause that many men may give you, but you will first finish your work that you have set yourself to perform, ere you give yourself ease to sit you down and to enjoy the fruits of your victory.

Yea, he who is a true king of men, will not say to himself, "Lo! I am worthy to be crowned with laurels;" but rather will he say to himself, "What more is there that I may do to make the world the better because of my endeavors?"

THE WINNING OF A QUEEN

crowned with laurels: Renowned, celebrated, distinguished.

$\mathfrak{N}$ow, the day was extraordinarily sweet and pleasant unto one so lusty of frame and so lithe of heart as was good King Arthur. For the bright clouds swam smoothly across the blue sky in prodigious volumes of vapor, and the wind blew across the long grass of the meadow lands, and across the fields of growing wheat, so that a multitude of waves travelled over the hills and valleys like an it were across an entire sea of green. And now all the earth would be darkened with wide shadows from those clouds, and, anon, everything would burst out, of a sudden, into a wonderful radiance of sunlight once more. And the little birds they sang all gayly in the hedge-rows and the leafy thickets as though they would burst their tiny throats with singing, and the cock crowed, strong and lusty, from the farm croft, and all was so blithe and comely that the young King, with the visor of his helmet uplifted to the refreshment of the gentle breeze, would sometimes carol very joyously in his journeying. So travelled King Arthur in all that gay and tender summer season, when the earth was young and time was of long-gone-by.

Now, you are to remember that when King Arthur had come from Carleon unto the castle of Tintagalon, he had brought with him four young knights for to bear him company. And those knights aforesaid were as follows: There was Sir Gawaine, the son of King Lot and of Queen Margaise, and there was Sir Ewaine, the son of King Urien and of Queen Morgana le Fay (and these two were nephews, half in

3

HOW KING ARTHUR ENCOUN-
TERED FOUR KNIGHTS AND
OF WHAT BEFELL THEREBY.

croft: A small piece of land worked by peasant farmers.

blood, unto the King), and there was Sir Pellias, and there was Sir Geraint, the son of Erbin. These were the four noble young knights who had come with King Arthur from Camelot unto Tintagalon.

Now it befell, as King Arthur rode all gayly in the summer time as aforesaid, that he came to a certain part of the road where he beheld before him a tall and comely tower that stood upon a green hillock immediately by the roadside. And lo! there stood upon the balcony of that tower three fair damoiselles, clad all in green taffeta. And on the high road in front of the castle there was a knight clad all in very fine armor. And the knight sat upon a noble war-horse, and in his hands he held a lute, and he played upon the lute and sang in a voice of extraordinary sweetness. Whiles he sang those three ladies in green taffeta listened to him with great cheerfulness of mien. And whenever that knight would stint his singing, then those three ladies would clap their hands together with great acclaim, and would bid him to sing to them again; and so he would do with great readiness of spirit.

All this King Arthur beheld, and it appeared to him to be a very pleasant sight, wherefore he rejoiced at it exceedingly.

And as he drew nigh, lo! he beheld that the knight who thus sat upon his horse and played upon the lute and sang unto the accompaniment thereof, was none other than Sir Geraint, the son of Erbin. For that knight wore upon his crest the figure of a gryphon, and the device upon his shield was two gryphons rampant facing one another upon a field azure, and King Arthur knew that this was the crest and the device of Sir Geraint. And when the King perceived who was the knight who sat there and sang, he laughed unto himself and straightway closed his visor and made him ready for such encounter as might, perchance, befall. So he drew nigh to where the knight sang and the ladies listened.

Now when Sir Geraint perceived King Arthur approach, he ceased singing and hung up his lute behind him across his

Lute

Two Gryphons Rampant

shoulder. Then, casting upward his look to those three fair ladies above him, quoth he: "Mesdames, ye have been pleased to listen to that singing which I have assayed altogether in your honor. Now, likewise, in your honor, I will perform a deed of knightly prowess which I very much hope shall bring great glory to you. For, if ye will be pleased to lend me that encouragement which your very great beauty can so easily afford, ye shall behold me, I doubt not, overthrow yonder knight completely, and that to your great credit and renown."

"Sir Knight," said that lady who spoke for the others, "you are, truly, a lord of noble bearing and exceedingly pleasing of address, wherefore we do wish you great success in this undertaking, and we do believe that you will succeed in that which you assay to do."

Upon these Sir Geraint gave those three damoiselles great thanks for their words, and thereupon he closed the visor of his helmet. So, dressing his spear and shield, and saluting those three ladies with great humility of demeanor, he went forth to meet King Arthur where he now sat at a little distance, very quietly and soberly awaiting his pleasure.

Now Sir Geraint knew not King Arthur because he wore no crest upon his helm and no device upon his shield, wherefore as he saluted him he made speech to him in this wise: "Ha! Messire, I know not who thou art, seeing that thou bearest neither crest nor device. Ne'theless, I am minded to do thee such honor as I may in running a tilt with thee upon the behalf of those three damoiselles whom thou beholdest yonder upon that balcony. For I do affirm, and am ready to maintain the same with my knightly person, that those ladies are fairer than thy lady, whomsoever she may be."

"Sir Knight," quoth King Arthur, "I will gladly run a course with thee in honor of my lady; for, I may tell thee, she is a princess, and is held by many to be the most

Mesdames: Ladies.

demeanor: Manner or behavior.

Messire: Sire; a title of honor for high-ranking nobles.

beautiful dame in all of the world. But I will only contend with thee upon one condition, and the condition is this—that he who is overthrown shall yield himself as servant unto the other for seven days, and in that time he shall do all that may be required of him."

"I will accept thy gage, Sir Unknown Knight," quoth Sir Geraint, "and when I have overthrown thee, I will yield thee unto those fair ladies yonder for to be their servant for seven days. And I do tell thee that there are a great many knights who would certainly regard that as being both a pleasant and an honorable task."

"And should I so chance as to overthrow thee," said King Arthur, "I will send thee for to serve my lady for that same period of time, and that will be even a pleasanter and a more honorable task than that which thou hast a mind for me to perform."

So each knight saluted the other, and thereupon each took such a stand as should cast the encounter immediately beneath where those three fair damoiselles looked down from the balcony. Then each knight dressed his spear and his shield, and, having made ready for the encounter, each sat for a small space entirely prepared. Then each shouted to his war-horse, and drave spur into its flank, and launched forth with wonderful speed to the assault. So they met in the very midst of the course with a force so vehement that the noise thereof was wonderfully appalling for to hear. And each knight smote the other in the very centre of his defences. And, lo! the spear of Sir Geraint burst into small pieces, even to the truncheon thereof; but the spear of King Arthur held, and Sir Geraint was cast so violently backward that both he and his horse were overthrown into the dust with a tumult like to a monstrous roaring of thunder.

And when Sir Geraint had recovered his footing, he was, for awhile, so astonished that he wist not where he stood, for never had he been so overthrown in all of his life before. Then, coming quickly unto himself again, he straightway

gage: A challenge.

132

drew forth his sword and called upon King Arthur with exceeding vehemence for to come down from out of his saddle, and to fight him afoot.

"Nay, not so, Sir Knight," said King Arthur, "I will not have to do with thee in that way. Moreover, thou art not to forget that thou hast promised to give thyself unto me as my servant for seven days, for, assuredly, I have entirely overcome thee in this encounter, and now thou art pledged unto me to be my servant."

Then Sir Geraint knew not what to say, being altogether abashed with shame and vexation at his overthrow. Ne'theless, he perceived that he must uphold his knightly word unto that which he had pledged himself to do; wherefore, he put up his sword again, though with exceeding discontent. "Sir Knight," said he, "I do acknowledge myself to have been overcome in this encounter, wherefore I yield myself now unto thy commands, according to my plighted word."

plighted: Pledged.

"Then I do place my commands upon thee in this wise," quoth King Arthur. "My command is, that thou goest straightway unto the Lady Guinevere at Cameliard, and that thou tellest her that thou hast been overthrown by that knight to whom she gave her necklace as a token. Moreover, I do desire that thou shalt obey her in everything that she may command thee to do, and that for the space of seven days to come."

"Sir Knight," quoth Sir Geraint, "that which thou biddest me to do, I will perform according to thy commands."

Thereupon he mounted his horse and went his way. And King Arthur went his way. And those three ladies who stood upon the balcony of the castle were exceedingly glad that they had beheld so noble an assay-at-arms as that which they had looked down upon.

Now, after King Arthur had travelled forward for the distance of two or three leagues or more, he came to a certain place of moorlands, where were many ditches of water, and

sedge: Coarse, grassy, rush-like plants that grow in wet places.

causeway: A raised way formed on a mound across low wet ground.
pollard willows: Willows that have either been cut back to produce a thick, close growth of young branches or whose branches have been cut off, leaving only the main trunk.

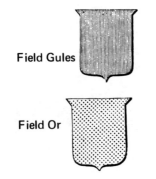

Field Gules

Field Or

where the heron and the marsh-hen sought harborage in the sedge. And here, at sundry points, were several windmills, with their sails all turning slowly in the sunlight before a wind which blew across the level plains of ooze. And at this place there was a long, straight causeway, with two long rows of pollard willows, one upon either hand. Now, when he had come nigh the middle of this causeway, King Arthur perceived two knights, who sat their horses in the shade of a great windmill that stood upon one side of the roadway. And a large shadow of the sails moved ever and anon across the roadway as the wheel of the mill turned slowly afore the wind. And all about the mill, and everywhere about, were great quantities of swallows that darted hither and thither like bees about a hive in midsummer. And King Arthur saw that those two knights, as they sat in the shadow of the mill, were eating of a great loaf of rye bread, fresh baked and of brittle crust; and they ate fair white cheese, which things the miller, all white with dust, served to them. But when these two knights perceived King Arthur, they immediately ceased eating that bread and cheese, and straightway closed their helmets. As for the miller, when he saw them thus prepare themselves, he went quickly back into the mill and shut the door thereof, and then went and looked out of a window which was over above where the knights were standing.

But King Arthur made very merry unto himself when he perceived that those two knights were Sir Gawaine and Sir Ewaine. For he knew that the one was Sir Gawaine because that the crest of his helmet was a leopard rampant, and because he bore upon his shield the device of a leopard rampant upon a field gules; and he knew that the other was Sir Ewaine, because he bore upon his crest an unicorn, and because the device upon his shield was that of a lady holding a naked sword in her hand, which same was upon a field or. Accordingly, whiles he was yet at some distance, King Arthur closed his helmet so that those two young knights might not know who he was.

So, when he had come anear to the two knights, Sir Gawaine rode forward for a little distance for to meet him. "Sir Knight," quoth he, "thou must know that this is soothly parlous ground whereon thou hast ventured; for there is no byway hence across the morass, and thou mayst not go forward without trying a tilt with me."

"Sir Knight," said King Arthur, "and I am very willing to run a tilt with thee. Ne'theless, I will only encounter thee upon one condition, and that is this: that he who is overthrown shall serve the other entirely for the space of seven full days."

"I do accept thy gage, Sir Knight," quoth Sir Gawaine. For he said unto himself, "Of a surety, so exceedingly strong and skilful a knight as I shall easily encompass the overthrow of this unknown knight."

So each knight immediately took his appointed station, and having dressed his spear and his shield, and having fully prepared himself in every manner, and having rested for a little space, each suddenly shouted to his horse, and drave spur into the flanks thereof, and so rushed to the encounter. And each knight smote the other in the midst of his defence, and lo! the spear of Sir Gawaine burst into fragments. But the spear of King Arthur held, so that Sir Gawaine was lifted entirely out of his saddle and over the crupper of his horse. And indeed he fell with wonderful violence into the dust. Nor could he immediately rise from that fall, but lay all bedazed for a little while. And when he did arise, he perceived that the white knight who had overthrown him sat nigh to him upon his horse.

Then King Arthur spake and said: "Sir Knight, I have altogether overthrown thee, and so thou must now serve me according to thy knightly word."

Then up spake Sir Ewaine, who sat nearby upon his horse. "Not so, Sir Knight," he said; "not so, nor until thou hast had to do with me. For I do make demand of thee that thou shalt straightway joust with me. And if I overthrow thee I will claim of thee that thou shalt release my cousin from that servitude unto which he hath pledged himself. But if thou overthrowst me, then will I serve thee even as he hath pledged himself to serve thee."

"Sir Knight," said King Arthur, "I do accept thy gage with all readiness of spirit!"

So each knight took his assigned place and dressed himself for the encounter. Then they shouted, and drave together, rushing the one upon the other like unto two rams upon the hillside. And the spear of Sir Ewaine was also shivered into

joust: To fight with lances from horseback. In such a contest between knights, each tried to unseat his opponent.

136

pieces. But King Arthur's spear held, so that the girths of Sir Ewaine's saddle were burst apart, and both the saddle and the knight were swept off the horse's back with such violence that a tower falling could not have made a greater noise than did Sir Ewaine when he smote the dust of that causeway.

Then Sir Ewaine arose to his feet and gazed upon him, all filled with entire amazement. To him came King Arthur, and bespake him thus: "Ha, Sir Knight, meseems that thou hast been fairly overcome this day. And so, according to your promises, both thou and yonder other knight must fulfil all my commands for the space of full seven days to come. Now this is the command that I set upon ye both: that ye shall straightway go unto the Lady Guinevere at Cameliard and shall take her greeting from her knight. And ye shall say to her that her knight unto whom she gave her necklace, hath sent ye, who are King's sons, for to do obedience unto her. And all that she shall command ye to do in the space of these seven days that are to come, that shall ye perform even unto the smallest grain."

"Sir Knight," said Sir Gawaine, "so we will do according to thy commands, having pledged ourselves thereunto. But when these seven days are passed, I do make my vow that I shall seek thee out and shall carry this combat unto its entire extremity. For it may happen to any knight to be unhorsed as I have been, yet I do believe that I may have a better success with thee an I battle with thee to the extremity of my endeavor."

extremity: Here, end.

"Sir Knight," said King Arthur, "it shall be even as thou desirest. Yet I do verily believe that when these seven days are passed thou wilt not have such a great desire for to fight with me as thou now hast."

Having so spoken, King Arthur saluted those two knights and they saluted him. And then he turned his horse and went his way. And whenever he bethought him of how those two good knights had fallen before his assault, and when he thought of how astonished and abashed they had been at their overthrow, he laughed aloud for pure mirth, and vowed unto himself that he had never in all of his life engaged in so joyous an adventure as this.

So when Sir Ewaine had mended the girths of his saddle then he and Sir Gawaine mounted their horses and betook their way toward Cameliard much cast down in spirits.

Then the miller came forth from the mill once more, greatly rejoiced at having beheld such a wonderfully knightly encounter from so safe a place as that from which he had beheld it.

And so King Arthur rode onward with great content of mind until the slanting of the afternoon had come, and by that time he had come nigh to that arm of the forest-land which he had in mind as the proper place where he might leave his horse and his armor.

gnarled: Twisted.

Now as he drew nigh to this part of the forest skirts, he perceived before him at the roadside a gnarled and stunted oak-tree. And he perceived that upon the oak-tree there hung a shield, and that underneath the shield were written these words in fair large letters:

> *"Whoso smiteth upon this shield*
> *Doeth so at the peril of his body."*

Then King Arthur was filled with a great spirit, and, uplifting his spear, he smote upon that shield so that it rang like thunder.

assail: Strike.

Then immediately King Arthur heard a voice issue out of the forest crying, "Who hath dared to assail my shield!" And straightway there came out thence a knight of large frame, riding upon a horse white, like that which King Arthur himself rode. And the trappings of the horse and of the knight were all white like unto the trappings of King Arthur and his horse. And the knight bore upon his helmet as his crest a swan with outspread wings, and upon his shield he bore the emblazonment of three swans upon a field argent. And because of the crest and the emblazonment of the shield, King Arthur knew that this knight was Sir Pellias, who had come with him from Camelot to Tintagalon.

So when Sir Pellias had come nigh to where King Arthur waited for him, he drew rein and bespake him with great sternness of voice: "Ho! Ho! Sir Knight," quoted he. "Why didst thou dare to smite upon my shield! Verily, that blow shall bring thee great peril and dole. Now, prepare to defend thyself straightway because of what thou hast done."

"Stay! Stay! Sir Knight," said King Arthur, "it shall be as thou wouldst have it; and I will do combat with thee. Yet will I not assay this adventure until thou hast agreed that the knight who is overcome in the encounter shall serve the other in whatsoever manner that other may desire, for the space of one se'night from this time."

"Sir Knight," said Sir Pellias, "I do accept that risk, wherefore I bid thee now presently to prepare thyself for the encounter."

Thereupon each knight took his station and dressed his spear and shield. And when they had prepared themselves, they immediately launched together with a violence like to two stones cast from a catapult. So they met in the midst of the course, and again King Arthur was entirely successful in that assault which he made. For the spear of Sir Pellias burst to pieces, and the spear of King Arthur held; and Sir Pellias was cast with passing violence out of his saddle for the distance of more than half a spear's length behind the crupper of his horse. Nor did he altogether recover from that fall for a long time, so that King Arthur had to wait beside him for a considerable while ere he was able to lift himself up from the ground whereon he lay.

"Ha! Sir Knight," said King Arthur, "assuredly it hath not gone well with thee this day, for thou hast been entirely

catapult: A weapon with a powerful thrust for hurling stones.

overthrown and now thou must straightway redeem thy pledge to serve me for seven days hereafter. Wherefore, I now set it upon thee as my command, that thou shalt go straightway unto Cameliard, and that thou shalt greet the Lady Guinevere from me, telling her that her knight unto whom she gave her necklace hath been successful in battle with thee. Likewise I set it upon thee that thou shalt obey her for the space of seven days in whatsoever she may command thee to do."

"Sir Knight," said Sir Pellias, "it shall even be as thou dost ordain. Yet I would that I knew who thou art, for I do declare that I have never yet in all my life been overthrown as thou hast overthrown me. And, indeed, I think that there are very few men in the world who could serve me as thou hast served me."

"Sir Knight," said King Arthur, "some time thou shalt know who I am. But, as yet, I am bound to entire secrecy."

Thereupon he saluted Sir Pellias and turned and entered the forest and was gone.

And Sir Pellias mounted his horse and betook him to Cameliard, much cast down and disturbed in spirit, yet much marvelling who that knight could be who had served him as he had been served.

So that day there came to Cameliard, first Sir Geraint and then Sir Gawaine and Sir Ewaine, and last of all there came Sir Pellias. And when these four beheld one another they were all abashed so that one scarce dared to look the other in the face. And when they came before the Lady Guinevere and made their condition known to her, and told her how that knight who wore her necklace had overthrown them all and had sent them thither to serve her for a se'night and when she reckoned how great and famous were those four knights in deeds of chivalry, she was exceedingly exalted that her knight should have approved himself so great in those deeds of arms which he had undertaken to perform. But she

abashed: Embarrassed.

se'night: A week; seven nights.

140

greatly marvelled who that champion could be, and debated those things in her own mind. For it was a thing altogether unheard of that one knight, in one day, and with a single spear, should have overthrown five such well proved and famous knights as Duke Mordaunt of North Umber, Sir Geraint, Sir Gawaine, Sir Ewaine, and Sir Pellias. So she gave herself great joy that she had bestowed the gift of her necklace upon so worthy a knight, and she was exceedingly uplifted with extraordinary pleasure at the thought of the credit he had endowed her withal.

Now after King Arthur had entered the forest, he came by and by to where those wood-choppers, afore spoken of, plied their craft. And he abided with them for that night; and when the next morning had come, he intrusted them with his horse and armor, charging them to guard those things with all care, and that they should be wonderfully rewarded therefor. Then he took his departure from that place with intent to return unto Cameliard. And he was clad in that jerkin of frieze which he had worn ever since he had left Tintagalon.

And when he had reached the outskirts of the forest, he set his cap of disguise upon his head and so resumed his mean appearance once more. So, his knightliness being entirely hidden, he returned to Cameliard for to be gardener's boy as he had been before.

plied: Worked busily or steadily at.

141

Now, when King Arthur returned to Cameliard once more (which fell upon the afternoon of a second day), he found the gardener waiting for him, exceedingly filled with wrath. And the gardener had a long birchen rod which he had fetched thither for to punish his boy withal, when that he should have returned to the garden again. So when he saw King Arthur he said: "Thou knave! wherefore didst thou quit thy work to go a-gadding?" And King Arthur laughed and said: "Touch me not." At this, the gardener waxed so exceeding wroth, that he catched the King by the collar of his jerkin with intent to beat him, saying: "Dost thou laugh at me, knave, and make a mock at me? Now I will beat thee well for the offence thou hast committed."

Then, when King Arthur felt that man's hand laid upon him, and when he heard the words that the gardener spake in his wrath, his royal spirit waxed very big within him and he cried out: "Ha, wretch! wouldst thou dare to lay thy hands upon my sacred person?" So saying, he seized the gardener by the wrists, and took the rod straight away from him, and struck him with it across the shoulders. And when that poor knave felt himself thus in the powerful grasp of the angry King, and when he felt the rod upon his shoulders, he straightway lifted up a great outcry, albeit the blow hurt him not a whit. "Now get thee gone!" quoth King Arthur, "and trouble me no more; else will I serve thee in a way that will not at all belike thee." Herewith he loosed that poor man and

4

HOW THE FOUR KNIGHTS SERVED THE LADY GUINE-VERE.

a-gadding: Wandering.

a whit: A jot, bit.

bemazed: Stunned.

let him go; and the gardener was so bemazed with terror, that both the earth and the sky swam before him. For King Arthur's eyes had flashed upon him like lightning, and those two hands had held his wrists with wonderful power. Wherefore, when the King let him go he gat him away as quickly as might be, all trembling and sweating with a great fear.

So he went straight to the Lady Guinevere and complained to her of the manner in which he had been treated. "Lady," quoth he, weeping with the memory of his terror, "my boy goeth away for a day or more, I know not whither; and when I would whip him for quitting his work he taketh the rod straight away from me and beateth me with it. Wherefore, now, I prithee, deal with him as is fitting, and let several strong men drive him away from this place with rods."

Then the Lady Guinevere laughed. "Let be!" she said, "and meddle with him no more; for, indeed, he appeareth to

saucy: Impertinent.

be a very saucy fellow. As for thee! take thou no heed of his coming or his going, and haply I will deal with him in such a way as shall be fitting."

Whereupon the gardener went his way, greatly marvelling that the Lady Guinevere should be so mild in dealing with

toward: Pert, cheeky, forward.

that toward knave. And the Lady Guinevere went her way, very merry. For she began to bethink her that there was soothly some excellent reason why it should happen that when the White Champion, who did such wonderful deeds, should come thither, then that gardener's boy should go; and that when that same Champion should go, then the gardener's boy should come thitherward again. Wherefore she suspected many things, and was wonderfully merry and cheerful of spirit.

Now, that day, in the afternoon, the Lady Guinevere chanced to walk in the garden with her damsels, and with her walked those four noble knights who had been sent thither by her White Champion, to wit, Sir Gawaine, Sir Ewaine, Sir Geraint, and Sir Pellias. And the gardener's lad was digging in

144

the gardens; and as they passed by where he was the Lady Guinevere laughed aloud and cried out: "Look! Look! Messires and Ladies! Yonder is a very saucy fellow for to be a gardener's lad, for he continually weareth his cap, even when he standeth in the presence of lords and ladies."

Then Sir Gawaine up and spake, saying: "Is it even so? Now will I straightway go to yonder knave, and will take his hat off for him, and that in a way so greatly to his misliking, that I do not believe that he will ever offend by wearing it in our presence again."

At this the Lady Guinevere laughed a very great deal. "Let be!" she said, "let be! Sir Gawaine! it would ill beseem one so gentle as thou art to have to do with yonder saucy fellow. Moreover, he doth assure us all that he hath an ugly place upon his head, wherefore let him wear his cap in God's mercy."

Thus the Lady Guinevere, though she suspected a very great deal, was yet pleased to make a mock of him whom she suspected.

Now that day Duke Mordaunt of North Umber had entirely recovered from those sore hurts that he had suffered from his overthrow at the hands of the White Champion. Wherefore, the next morning having come, he appeared again before the castle as he had appeared aforetime— clad all in complete armor. So this time there rode before him two heralds, and when the duke and the two heralds had come to that part of the meadows that lay immediately before the castle of Cameliard, the heralds blew their trumpets exceedingly loud. So at the sound of the trumpets many people came and gathered upon the walls; and King Leodegrance came, and took stand upon a lesser tower that looked down upon the plain where were the Duke of North Umber and the two heralds. Then the Duke of North Umber lifted up his eyes and beheld King Leodegrance where he stood over above him upon the top of that tower, and he cried out in a loud voice: "What ho! King Leodegrance! Thou shalt not think because I suffered a fall from my horse through the mischance of an assault at arms, that thou art therefore quit of me. Yet, ne'theless, I do now make this fair proffer unto thee. To-morrow day I shall appear before this castle with six knights-companion. Now if thou hast any seven knights who are able to stand against me and my companions in an assault at arms—whether with spears or swords, or ahorse or afoot—then shall I engage myself for to give over all pretence whatsoever unto the hand of the Lady Guinevere. But if thou canst not provide such champions to contend successfully against me and my knights-companion, then shall I not only lay claim to Lady Guinevere, but I shall likewise seize upon and shall hold for mine own, three certain castles of thine that stand upon the borders of North Umber. And, likewise, I shall seize upon and shall hold for mine own all the lands and glebes appertaining unto those same castles. Moreover, this challenge of mine shall hold only until to-morrow at set of sun; after the which time it shall be null and void. Wherefore, King Leodegrance, thou hadst best look to it straightway to provide thee with such champions as may defend thee from these demands aforesaid."

glebes: Farm land.

Hereupon those two heralds blew their trumpets once more, and Duke Mordaunt of North Umber turned his horse about and went away from that place. Then King Leodegrance also went his way, very sorrowful and downcast in his spirits. For he said to himself: "Is it at all likely that another champion shall come unto me like that wonderful White Champion who came two days since, I know not whence, for to defend me against mine enemies? And, touching that same White Champion; if I know not whence he came, so also I know not whither he hath departed; how then shall I know where to seek him to beseech his further aid in this time of mine extremity?" Wherefore he went his way, very sorrowful, and wist not what he was to do for to defend himself. So being thus exceedingly troubled in his spirit, he went straight unto his own room, and there shut

extremity: Here, extreme need.

146

himself therein; nor would he see any man nor speak unto anyone, but gave himself over entirely unto sorrow and despair.

Now in this extremity the Lady Guinevere bethought her of those four knights who had been pledged for to serve her for seven days. So she went unto them where they were and she bespoke them in this wise: "Messires, ye have been sent hither pledged for to serve me for seven days. Now I do ordain it of thee that you will take this challenge of Duke Mordaunt upon you at my behest, and I do much desire that you go forth to-morrow-day for to meet this Duke of North Umber and his knights-companion in battle. For ye are terribly powerful knights, and I do believe you may easily defend us against our enemies."

But Sir Gawaine said, "Not so, Lady; not so! For though we are pledged unto thy service, yet are we not pledged unto the service of King Leodegrance, thy father. Nor have we quarrel of any sort with this Duke of North Umber, nor with his six knights-companion. For we are knights of King Arthur, his Court, nor may we, except at his command, take any foreign quarrel upon us in the service of another king."

Then was the Lady Guinevere exceedingly angry, wherefore she said with great heat: "Either thou art a wonderfully faithful lord unto thy King, Sir Gawaine, or else thou fearest to meet this Duke of North Umber and his knights-companion."

heat: Excitement, emotion, feeling.

And at this speech of the Lady Guinevere's, Sir Gawaine was also exceedingly wroth, wherefore he made reply: "An thou wert a knight and not a lady, Dame Guinevere, thou wouldst think three or four times ere thou wouldst find courage to speak those words unto me." Whereupon he arose and went out from that place with a countenance all inflamed with wrath. And the Lady Guinevere went away also from that place and to her bower, where she wept a very great deal, both from sorrow and from anger.

Now all this while King Arthur had been very well aware

of everything that passed; wherefore he by and by arose and went out and found the gardener. And he took the gardener strongly by the collar of his coat and held him where he was. And he said to him: "Sirrah! I have a command to set upon thee, and thou shalt perform that command to the letter, else, an thou perform it not, a very great deal of pain may befall thee." Herewith speaking, he thrust his hand into the bosom of his jerkin and brought forth thence that necklace of pearls which the Lady Guinevere had given him from about her neck. And he said further unto the gardener: "Thou shalt take this necklace to the Lady Guinevere and thou shalt say to her thus: that she is to send me forthwith bread and meat and wine and comfits from her own table. And thou shalt say unto her that I desire her to summon those four knights—to wit, Sir Gawaine, Sir Ewaine, Sir Geraint, and Sir Pellias—and that she is to bid those four for to come and serve me with those things for my refreshment. And thou art to say unto her that she is to lay her commands upon those knights that they are further to serve me according as I may command, and that they are henceforth to be my servants and not her servants. And these are the commands that I lay upon thee; that thou art to say these things unto the Lady Guinevere."

Now when the gardener heard those words he was so astonished that he wist not what to think, for he deemed that the gardener's lad had gone altogether mad. Wherefore he lifted up his voice and cried aloud, "How now! What is this thou sayest! Verily, should I do such a thing as this thou bidst me to do, either it will cost me my life or else it will cost thee thy life. For who would dare for to say such words unto the Lady Guinevere?"

But King Arthur said: "Ne'theless, thou shalt surely do as I command thee, sirrah. For if thou disobey in one single point, then I do assure thee it will go exceedingly ill with thee. For I have it in my power for to make thee suffer as thou hast never suffered before."

148

And upon this the gardener said, "I will go." For he said unto himself, "If I do as this fellow biddeth me, then will the Lady Guinevere have him punished in great measure, and so I shall be revenged upon him for what he did unto me yesterday. Moreover, it irks me exceedingly that I should have a lad for to work in the garden who behaves as this fellow does. Wherefore," he said, "I will go." So he took that necklace of pearls that King Arthur gave him, and he went forth and, after awhile, he found the Lady Guinevere where she was. And when he had found her, he bespoke her in this wise:

sweetmeats: Candied fruit or any sweet food, like cake or candy, that is made with sugar or honey.

dire: Serious.

sin: A Scottish word for since.

"Lady, my garden boy hath assuredly gone entirely mad. For, under the threat of certain great harm he would do unto me an I performed not his errand, he hath sent me to offer a very grievous affront unto thee. For he hath sent me with this string of large beads for to give to thee; and he bids me to tell thee that thou art to send to him bread and meat and sweetmeats and wine, such as thou usest at thine own table; and he bids me to tell thee that these things are to be served to him by the four noble knights who came hither the day before yesterday. And he saith that thou art to command those same knights that they are to obey him in whatsoever he may command, for that they are henceforth to be his servants and not thine. And, indeed, Lady, he would listen to naught that I might say to him contrariwise, but he hath threatened me with dire injury an I came not hither and delivered this message unto thee."

Now when the Lady Guinevere heard what the gardener said, and when she beheld the necklace which she had given unto that White Champion, and when she wist that the White Champion and the gardener's boy were indeed one, she was uplifted with an exceeding joy; wherefore she knew not whether to laugh or whether to weep for that pure joy. So she arose and took the necklace of pearls, and she bade the gardener for to come with her. Then she went forth until she found those four knights, and when she had found them she spake unto them thus:

"My Lords, awhile sin when I commanded you for to take my quarrel with Duke Mordaunt of North Umber upon you for my sake, ye would not do so. And thou, my lord Gawaine, didst speak such angry words as are not fitting that one who serveth should speak unto his mistress, far less that a knight should speak unto the daughter of a king. Accordingly I have it in my mind that ye shall perform a certain thing by way of a penance, which, an ye refuse to do, I will know very well that ye do not intend to fulfil that word which ye plighted to my knight when he overthrew you all four in fair combat. Now my command is this: that ye take certain food prepared for my table—meats and white bread and sweetmeats and wine—and that ye take that food unto my gardener's boy, whose cap, Sir Gawaine, thou didst threaten so valorously for to take away from him this very morning. And ye four are to serve the food unto him as though he were a royal knight. And when ye have so served him, ye are to obey him in whatsoever he may ordain. And this I put upon ye as a penalty because ye took not my quarrel upon ye as true knights should, for hereafter ye are to be servants unto that gardener's boy and not unto me. Wherefore ye are now to go unto the buttery of the castle, and ye are to bid the sewer for to give you meats such as are served upon mine own table. And the food ye are to serve upon silver plates, and the wine ye are to serve in silver cups and goblets. And ye are to minister unto that gardener's boy as though he were a great lord of exceeding fame and renown."

Thus spake the Lady Guinevere, and when she had spoken, she turned and left those four knights, and she took with her the gardener, who was so astonished at that which he had heard, that he wist not whether he had gone mad or whether the Lady Guinevere had gone mad. And the Lady Guinevere bade the gardener to go to the gardener's boy and to tell him that all things should be fulfilled according to his commands. And so the gardener did as he was told.

Now turn we to those four knights whom the Lady Guinevere had left. For they were bemazed and abashed at the singular commands she had set upon them. And when they recovered from their amazement, they were inflamed with exceeding indignation that, for the time, they wist not whether that which they saw with their eyes was the light of day, or whether it was altogether darkness. Nor could one of them look at another in the face, so overcome were they with shame at the affront that had been put upon them. Then up

buttery: The pantry.

sewer (soo-er): A high-ranking servant charged with serving meals.

and spake Sir Gawaine, and his voice so trembled with his exceeding anger that he could scarce contain it for to speak his words. "Messires," quoth he, "do ye not see how that this lady hath wantonly put a great affront upon us because we would not do that which she this morning bade us to do, and because we would not take up her quarrel against the Duke of North Umber? Now we will indeed serve this gardener's boy even as she hath ordained. For we will serve him with meat and drink as she hath commanded; and we will render our service unto him as she hath bidden us to do. But observe ye; we are no longer her servants, but we are his servants; wherefore we may serve him as we choose for to do. So, when we have fulfilled her commands and have served him with meat and drink, and when we have obeyed all the behests he layeth upon us; then do I make my vow that I, with mine own hand, shall slay that gardener's boy. And when I have slain him, I will put his head into a bag, and I will send that bag unto the Lady Guinevere by the meanest carrier whom I can find for that purpose. And so this proud lady shall receive an affront as great as that affront which she hath put upon us." And they all said that that which Sir Gawaine had planned should be exactly as he had said.

So those four lords went unto the sewer of the castle, and they asked for the best of that food which was to be served unto the Lady Guinevere—meats and bread and sweetmeats and wine. Then they took them silver plates and platters and they placed the food upon them; and they took silver cups and silver goblets and they poured the wine into them; and they went forth with these things. And when they had come back of the castle nigh to the stables, they found the gardener's boy, and they bade him sit down and eat and to drink. And they waited upon him as though he had been some great lord. And not one of those four knights wist who he was, nor that he was the great King whose servant they, soothly, were. For he wore his cap of disguise upon his head, wherefore they deemed him to be only a poor peasant fellow.

meanest: Here, lowliest.

Now when Sir Ewaine beheld that he still wore his cap before them, he spake unto him with great indignation, saying: "Ha, villain! Wouldst thou wear thy cap even in the presence of great princes and lords such as we be?"

Unto this Sir Gawaine said, "Let be, it matters not." And then he said very bitterly unto the gardener's boy: "Eat thou well, sirrah! For thou shalt hardly eat another meal of food upon this earth."

To this the gardener's boy made reply: "Sir Knight, that, haply, shall lie unto another will than thine for to determine. For maybe, I shall eat many other meals than this. And, maybe, ye shall serve at them as ye are serving me now." And those four lords were astonished beyond measure that he should bespeak them thus so calmly and without any appearance of fear.

Then, after he had eaten, the gardener's boy said unto those knights, "Behold, Messires, I have had enough and am done; and now I have other commands for you to fulfil. And my next command is that ye shall make ready straightway to go abroad with me, and to that end ye shall clothe yourselves with complete armor. And thou, Sir Gawaine, shalt go to the head stable-keeper of this castle, and thou shalt demand of him that he shall make ready the Lady Guinevere's palfrey so that I may straightway ride forth upon it. And when ye are all encased in your armor, and when everything is duly appointed according to my command, ye shall bring that palfrey unto the postern gate of the castle, and there I shall meet ye for to ride forth with you."

And Sir Gawaine said: "It shall be done in every way according as thou dost command. But when we ride forth from this castle it shall be a sorry journey for thee."

And the gardener's boy said: "I think not so, Sir Gawaine."

Then those four went away and did according as the gardener's boy commanded. And when they had made themselves ready in full array of armor, and when they had

THE WINNING
OF A QUEEN

Armor and Equipment for Man
and Horse, about 1290

Complete Armor of 1195-1205

obtained the Lady Guinevere's palfrey, they went unto the postern gate and there the gardener's boy met them. And when he saw that they sat their horses and that they moved not at his coming, he said: "Ha, Messires! would ye so entreat him whom ye have been ordained to serve? Now I do bid ye, Sir Gawaine and Sir Ewaine, for to come down and to hold my stirrup for me; and I bid ye, Sir Geraint and Sir Pellias, for to come down and to hold my palfrey for me whiles I mount."

Then those four noble knights did as they were commanded. And Sir Gawaine said: "Thou mayst command as thou dost list, and I do bid thee to make the most of it whiles thou mayst do so; for thou shalt have but a little while longer for to enjoy the great honor that hath fallen upon thee. For that honor which hath fallen upon thee—lo! it shall presently crush thee unto death."

And the gardener's boy said: "Not so; I believe I shall not die yet whiles." And again those four lords were greatly astonished at the calmness of his demeanor.

And so they rode forth from that place; and the gardener's boy would not permit that they should ride either before him or beside him, but he commanded them that they should ride behind him whiles they were still servants unto him.

So they rode as he assigned them for a considerable way. Then after they had gone forward a great distance, they drew nigh to a gloomy and dismal woodland that lay entirely beyond the country coadjacent to Cameliard. Then, when they had come nigh unto this woodland, Sir Gawaine rode a little forward, and he said: "Sir Gardener's Boy, seest thou yonder woodland? Now when we come into it thou shalt immediately die, and that by a sword that hath never yet been touched by any but noble or knightly blood."

And King Arthur turned him about in his saddle, and he said: "Ha! Sir Gawaine! Wouldst thou ride forward thus when I bid thee to ride behind me?"

list: Please.

And as he spake he took the cap from off his head, and, lo! they all beheld that it was King Arthur who rode with them.

Then a great silence of pure astonishment fell upon them all, and each man sat as though he were turned into an image of stone. And it was King Arthur who first spake. And he said: "Ha! how now, Sir Knights? Have ye no words of greeting for to pay to me? Certes, ye have served me with a very ill grace this day. Moreover, ye have threatened to slay me; and now, when I speak to you, ye say naught in reply."

Then those four knights immediately cried out aloud; and they leaped down from off their horses, and they kneeled down into the dust of the road. And when King Arthur beheld them kneeling there, he laughed with great joyfulness of spirit, and he bade them for to mount their horses again, for the time was passing by when there was much to do.

So they mounted their horses and rode away, and as they journeyed forward the King told them all that had befallen him, so that they were greatly amazed, and gave much acclaim unto the knightliness with which he had borne himself in those excellent adventures through which he had passed. And they rejoiced greatly that they had a king for to rule over them who was possessed of such a high and knightly spirit.

So they rode to that arm of the forest where King Arthur had left his horse and his armor.

acclaim: Praise, approval.

ow, when the next day had come, the Duke of North Umber and six knights-companion appeared upon the field in front of the castle of Cameliard as he had duly declared that he and they would do. And those seven champions appeared in very great estate; for in front of them there rode seven heralds with trumpets and tabards, and behind them there rode seven esquires, each esquire bearing the spear, the shield, the crest, and the banneret of the knight who was his lord and master. And the seven heralds blew their trumpets so exceedingly loud that the sound thereof penetrated unto the utmost parts of Cameliard, so that the people came running from everywhere. And while the heralds blew their trumpets the seven esquires shouted, and waved the spears and the bannerets. So those seven knights rode in such proud estate that those who looked upon them had hardly ever beheld such a splendid presentment of chivalry.

So they paraded up and down that field three times for its entire length, and, meantime, a great crowd of people, called thither by the blowing of the herald's trumpets, stood upon the walls and gazed therefrom at that noble spectacle. And all the Court of King Ryence came, and stood upon the plain in front of the King's pavilion, and they shouted and cheered the Duke of North Umber and his six knights-companion.

Meanwhile, King Leodegrance of Cameliard was so cast down with trouble and shame that he did not choose to show his face, but hid himself away from all his Court. Nor would he permit anyone for to come into his presence at that time.

Nevertheless, the Lady Guinevere, with sundry of her

5

HOW KING ARTHUR OVER-
CAME THE ENEMIES OF
KING LEODEGRANCE, AND
HOW HIS ROYALTY WAS
PROCLAIMED.

tabards: The official cloaks of heralds. They are emblazoned with the master's coat of arms and worn on special occasions.

damsels, went unto the King's closet where he was, and knocked upon the door thereof, and when the King denied her to come in to him, she spake to him through the door, giving him words of good cheer, saying: "My lord King and father, I prithee for to look up and to take good cheer unto thyself. For I do assure thee that there is one who hath our cause in his hands, and that one is, certes, a very glorious champion. And he shall assuredly come by and by ere this day is done, and when he cometh, he shall certainly overthrow our enemies."

But King Leodegrance opened not the door, but he said: "My daughter, that which thou sayest thou sayest for to comfort me. For there is no other help for me in this time of trouble only God, His good strong help and grace." And she said: "Nay, I say that which is the truth; and the help that God shall send unto thee he shall certainly send through a worthy champion who at this moment hath our cause in his hand."

So spake the Lady Guinevere, so that whilst King Leodegrance came not forth, yet he was greatly comforted at that which she said to him.

Thus passed all that morning and a part of the afternoon, and yet no one appeared for to take up that challenge which the seven knights had declared. But, whilst the sun was yet three or four hours high, there suddenly appeared at a great distance a cloud of dust. And in that cloud of dust there presently appeared five knights, riding at great speed, thitherward. And when these had come nigh unto the walls, lo! the people beheld that he who rode foremost of all was that same White Champion who had aforetime overthrown the Duke of North Umber. Moreover, they perceived that the four knights who rode with that White Champion were very famous knights and of great prowess and glory of arms. For the one was Sir Gawaine, and the other was Sir Ewaine, and the other was Sir Geraint, and the other was Sir Pellias. For the people of the castle and the town knew those four knights, because they had dwelt for two days at Cameliard, and they were of such exceeding renown that folk crowded from far and near for to look upon them whensoever they appeared for to walk abroad.

So when the people upon the walls beheld who those knights were, and when they perceived that White Champion who had aforetime brought them such exceeding honor, they shouted aloud for the second time with a voice mightier than that with which they had the first time shouted.

Now King Leodegrance heard the people shouting, whereupon hope awoke of a sudden within him. So he straightway came forth with all speed for to see what was ado, and there he beheld those five noble champions about to enter into the field below the castle walls.

And the Lady Guinevere also heard the shouting and she came forth likewise and, behold! there was that White Champion and those four other knights. So when she beheld that White Knight and his four companions-at-arms, her heart was like to break within her for pure joy and gladness, wherefore she wept for the passion thereof, and laughed the whiles she wept. And she waved her kerchief unto those five noble lords and kissed her hand unto them, and the five knights saluted her as they rode past her and into the field.

Now, when the Duke of North Umber was made aware that those five knights had come against him and his knights-companion for to take up his challenge, he straightway came forth from his pavilion and mounted his horse. And his knights-companion came forth and mounted their horses, and he and they went forth for to meet those who had come against them.

And when the Duke of North Umber had come nigh enough, he perceived that the chiefest of those five knights was the White Champion who had aforetime overthrown him. Wherefore he said unto that White Champion: "Sir Knight, I have once before condescended unto thee who art altogether unknown to me or to anybody else that is here. For without

condescended unto thee: Come down to your level.

inquiring concerning thy quality, I ran a course with thee and, lo! by the chance of arms thou didst overthrow me. Now this quarrel is more serious than that, wherefore I and my companions-at-arms will not run a course with thee and thy companions; nor will we fight with thee until I first know what is the quality of him against whom I contend. Wherefore, I bid thee presently declare thyself, who thou art and what is thy condition."

Then Sir Gawaine opened the umbril of his helmet, and he said: "Sir Knight, behold my face, and know that I am Gawaine, the son of King Lot. Wherefore thou mayst perceive that my condition and estate are even better than thine own. Now I do declare unto thee that yonder White Knight is of such a quality that he condescends unto thee when he doeth combat with thee, and that thou dost not condescend unto him."

"Ho, Sir Gawaine!" quoth the Duke of Umber. "What thou sayest is a very strange thing, for, indeed, there are few in this world who are so exalted that they may condescend unto me. Ne'theless, since thou dost avouch for him, I may not gainsay that which thou sayest. Yet, there is still another reason why we may not fight with ye. For, behold! we are seven well-approved and famous knights, and ye are but five; so, consider how unequal are our forces, and that you stand in great peril in undertaking so dangerous an encounter."

Then Sir Gawaine smiled right grimly upon that Duke of North Umber. "Gramercy for thy compassion, and for the tenderness which thou showeth concerning our safety, Sir Duke," quoth he. "But ne'theless, thou mayst leave that matter unto us with entire content of spirit upon thy part. For I consider that the peril in which ye seven stand is fully equal to our peril. Moreover, wert thou other than a belted knight, a simple man might suppose that thou wert more careful of thine own safety in this matter, than thou art of ours."

Now at these words the countenance of the Duke of North

avouch for: Affirm or speak for.
gainsay: Deny.

160

Umber became altogether covered with red, for he wist that he had, indeed, no great desire for this battle, wherefore he was ashamed because of the words which Sir Gawaine spake to him. So, each knight closed his helmet, and all turned their horses, and the one party rode unto one end of the field, and the other party rode to the other end of the field, and there each took stand in the place assigned unto them.

And they arranged themselves thus: In the middle was King Arthur, and upon either hand were two knights; and in the middle was the Duke of North Umber, and upon either hand were three knights. So, when they had thus arrayed themselves they dressed their spears and their shields, and made them altogether ready for the onset. Then King Arthur and Duke Mordaunt each shouted aloud, and the one party hurled upon the other party with such violence that the ground shook and thundered beneath the hoofs of the horses, and the clouds of dust rose up against the heavens.

And so they met in the middle of the field with an uproar of such dreadful violence that one might have heard the crashing thereof for the distance of more than a mile away.

And when the one party had passed the other, and the dust of the encounter had arisen, lo! three of the seven had been overthrown, and not one of the five had lost his seat.

And one of those who had been overthrown was Duke Mordaunt of North Umber. And, behold! he never more arose again from the ground whereon he lay. For King Arthur had directed his spear into the very midst of his defences, and the spear had held, wherefore the point thereof had pierced the shield of the Duke of North Umber, and had pierced his body armor, and so violent was the stroke, that the Duke of North Umber had been lifted entirely out of his saddle, and had been cast a full spear's length behind the crupper of his horse. Thus died that wicked man, for as King Arthur drave past him, the evil soul of him quitted his body with a weak noise like to the squeaking of a bat, and the world was well rid of him.

quitted: Left.

coil: Tumult; trouble.

Now when King Arthur turned him about at the end of the course and beheld that there were but four knights left upon their horses of all those seven against whom he and his companions had driven, he uplifted his spear, and drew rein upon his horse, and bespake his knights in this wise: "Messires, I am aweary of all this coil and quarrelling, and do not care to fight any more to-day, so go ye straightway and engage those knights in battle. As for me, I will abide here, and witness your adventure."

162

"Lord," said they, "we will do our endeavor as thou dost command."

So those four good knights did as he commanded, and they went forth straightway against those other four, much encouraged that their King looked upon their endeavor. And King Arthur sat with the butt of his spear resting upon his instep, and looked upon the field with great content of spirit, and a steadfast countenance.

As for those four knights-companion that remained of the Duke of North Umber's party, they came not forth to this second encounter with so much readiness of spirit as they had done aforetime. For they were now well aware of how great was the excellent prowess of those other knights, and they beheld that their enemies came forth to this second encounter very fiercely, and with great valor and readiness of spirit. Wherefore their hearts melted away within them with doubt and anxiety as to the outcome of this second encounter.

Nevertheless, they prepared themselves with such resolve as might be, and came forth as they were called upon to do.

Then Sir Gawaine drave straight up to the foremost knight, who was a very well-known champion, hight Sir Dinador of Montcalm. And when he had come sufficiently nigh to him, he lifted himself up in his stirrups and he smote Sir Dinador so fierce a blow that he cleft the shield of that knight asunder, and he cleft his helmet, and a part of the blade of his sword brake away and remained therein.

And when Sir Dinador felt that blow, his brains swam like water, and he was fain to catch the horn of his saddle for to save himself from falling therefrom. Then a great terror straightway fell upon him, so that he drew rein violently to one side. So he fled away from that place with the terror of death hanging above him like to a black cloud of smoke. And when his companions beheld that stroke that Sir Gawaine delivered, and when they beheld Sir Dinador flee away from

fain: Compelled, forced.

like chaff: Like straws or grain husks, which are lightweight and easily stirred by the wind.

Drawbridge

before him, they also drew rein to one side and fled away with all speed, pursued with an entire terror of their enemies. And Sir Gawaine and Sir Ewaine and Sir Geraint and Sir Pellias pursued them as they fled. And they chased them straight through the Court of King Ryence, so that the knights and nobles of that Court scattered hither and thither like chaff at their coming. And they chased those fleeing knights in among the pavilions of King Ryence's Court, and no man stayed them; and when they had chased those knights entirely away, they returned to that place where King Arthur still held his station, steadfastly awaiting them.

Now when the people of Cameliard beheld the overthrow of their enemies, and when they beheld how those enemies fled away from before the faces of their champions, they shouted with might and main, and made great acclaim. Nor did they stint their loud shouting when those four knights returned from pursuing their enemies and came back unto the White Champion again. And still more did they give acclaim when those five knights rode across the drawbridge and into the gateway of the town and into the town.

Thus ended the great bout-at-arms, which was one of the most famous in all the history of chivalry of King Arthur's Court.

Now when King Arthur had thus accomplished his purposes, and when he had come into the town again, he went unto that merchant of whom he had obtained the armor that he wore, and he delivered that armor back to him again. And he said, "To-morrow-day, Sir Merchant, I shall send thee two bags of gold for the rent of that armor which thou didst let me have."

To this the merchant said: "Lord, it is not needed that thou shouldst recompense me for that armor, for thou hast done great honor unto Cameliard by thy prowess."

But King Arthur said: "Have done, Sir Merchant, nor must thou forbid what I say. Wherefore take thou that which I shall send unto thee."

Thereupon he went his way, and, having set his cap of disguise upon his head, he came back into the Lady Guinevere's gardens again.

Now when the next morning had come the people of Cameliard looked forth and, lo! King Ryence had departed entirely away from before the castle. For that night he had struck his pavilions, and had withdrawn his Court, and had gone away from that place where he and his people had sat down for five days past. And with him he had taken the body of the Duke of North Umber, conveying it away in a litter surrounded by many lighted candles and uplifted by a peculiar pomp of ceremony. But when the people of Cameliard beheld that he was gone, they were exceedingly rejoiced, and made merry, and shouted and sang and laughed. For they wist not how deeply enraged King Ryence was against them; for his enmity aforetime toward King Leodegrance was but as a small flame when compared unto the anger that now possessed him.

Now that morning Lady Guinevere walked into her garden, and with her walked Sir Gawaine and Sir Ewaine, and lo! there she beheld the gardener's boy again.

Then she laughed aloud, and she said unto those two knights, "Messires behold! Yonder is the gardener's boy, who weareth his cap continually because he hath an ugly place upon his head."

Then those two knights, knowing who that gardener's boy was, were exceedingly abashed at her speech, and wist not what to say or whither to look. And Sir Gawaine spake, aside unto Sir Ewaine, and quoth he: " 'Fore Heaven, that lady knoweth not what manner of man is yonder gardener's boy; for, an she did, she would be more sparing of her speech."

And the Lady Guinevere heard Sir Gawaine that he spoke, but she did not hear his words. So she turned unto Sir Gawaine, and she said: "Sir Gawaine, haply it doth affront thee that that gardener's boy should wear his cap before us,

haply: Perhaps.

165

and maybe thou wilt go and take it off from his head as thou didst offer to do two or three days since."

And Sir Gawaine said: "Peace, Lady! Thou knowest not what thou sayest. Yonder gardener's boy could more easily take my head from off my shoulders than I could take his cap from off his head."

At this the Lady Guinevere made open laughter; but in her heart she secretly pondered that saying and greatly marvelled what Sir Gawaine meant thereby.

Now about noon of that day there came an herald from King Ryence of North Wales, and he appeared boldly before King Leodegrance where the King sat in his hall with a number of his people about him. And the herald said: "My lord King: my master, King Ryence of North Wales, is greatly displeased with thee. For thou didst set certain knights upon Duke Mordaunt of North Umber, and those knights have slain that excellent nobleman, who was close kin unto King Ryence. Moreover, thou hast made no reply to those demands that my master, King Ryence, hath made touching the delivery unto him of certain lands and castles bordering upon North Wales. Wherefore my master is affronted with thee beyond measure. So my master, King Ryence, bids me to set forth to thee two conditions, and the conditions are these: Firstly, that thou dost immediately deliver into his hands that White Knight who slew the Duke of North Umber; secondly, that thou makest immediate promise that those lands in question shall be presently delivered unto King Ryence."

Then King Leodegrance arose from where he sat and spake to that herald with great dignity of demeanor. "Sir Herald," quoth he, "the demands that King Ryence maketh upon me pass all bounds for insolence. That death which the Duke of North Umber suffered, he suffered because of his own pride and folly. Nor would I deliver that White Knight into thy

insolence: Arrogance, very rude behavior.

master's hands, even an I were able to do so. As for those lands that thy master demandeth of me, thou mayst tell King Ryence that I will not deliver unto him of those lands so much as a single blade of grass, or a single grain of corn that groweth thereon."

And the herald said: "If, so be, that is thine answer, King Leodegrance, then am I bidden for to tell thee that my master, King Ryence of North Wales, will presently come hither with an array of a great force of arms, and will take from thee by force those things which thou wilt not deliver unto him peacefully." Whereupon, so saying, he departed thence and went his way.

Now after the herald had departed, King Leodegrance went into his closet, and when he had come there he sent, privily, for the Lady Guinevere. So the Lady Guinevere came to him where he was. And King Leodegrance said to her: "My daughter, it hath happened that a knight clad all in white, and bearing no crest or device of any sort, hath twice come to our rescue and hath overthrown our enemies. Now it is said by everybody that that knight is thine own particular champion, and I hear say that he wore thy necklace as a favor when he first went out against the Duke of North Umber. Now I prithee, daughter, tell me who that White Champion is, and where he may be found."

Then the Lady Guinevere was overwhelmed with a confusion, wherefore she looked away from her father's countenance; and she said: "Verily, my Lord, I know not who that knight may be."

Then King Leodegrance spake very seriously to the Lady Guinevere, and he took her by the hand and said: "My daughter, thou art now of an age when thou must consider being mated unto a man who may duly cherish thee and protect thee from thine enemies. For, lo! I grow apace in years, and may not hope to defend thee always from those perils that encompass one of our estate. Moreover, since King

cherish: Tenderly care for.

167

Arthur (who is a very great King indeed) hath brought peace unto this realm, all that noble court of chivalry which one time gathered about me has been scattered elsewhither where greater adventures may be found than in my peaceful realm. Wherefore (as all the world hath seen this week past) I have now not one single knight whom I may depend upon to defend us in such times of peril as these which now overshadow us. Now, my daughter, it doth appear to me that thou couldst not hope to find anyone who could so well safeguard thee as this White Knight; for he doth indeed appear to be a champion of extraordinary prowess and strength. Wherefore it would be well if thou didst feel thyself to incline unto him as he appeareth to incline unto thee."

Then the Lady Guinevere became all rosy red as with a fire even unto her throat. And she laughed, albeit the tears overflowed her eyes and ran down upon her cheeks. So she wept, yet laughed in weeping. And she said unto King Leodegrance: "My Lord and father, an I give my liking unto any one in the manner thou speaketh of, I will give it only unto the poor gardener's boy who digs in my garden."

Then, at these words, the countenance of King Leodegrance became contracted with violent anger, and he cried out: "Ha, Lady! Wouldst thou make a mock and a jest of my words?"

Then the Lady Guinevere said: "Indeed, my Lord! I jest not and I mock not. Moreover, I tell thee for verity that that same gardener's boy knoweth more concerning the White Champion than anybody else in all of the world." Then King Leodegrance said: "What is this that thou tellest me?" And the Lady Guinevere said: "Send for that gardener's boy and thou shalt know." And King Leodegrance said: "Verily, there is more in this than I may at present understand."

So he called to him the chief of his pages, hight Dorisand, and he said to him: "Go, Dorisand, and bring hither the gardener's boy from the Lady Guinevere's garden."

jest: A joke.

168

So Dorisand, the page, went as King Leodegrance commanded, and in a little while he returned, bringing with him
that gardener's boy. And with them came Sir Gawaine, and
Sir Ewaine, and Sir Pellias and Sir Geraint. And those four
lords stood over against the door, where they entered; but
the gardener's boy came and stood beside the table where
King Leodegrance sat. And the King lifted up his eyes and
looked upon the gardener's boy, and he said: "Ha! Wouldst
thou wear thy cap in our presence?"

Then the gardener's boy said: "I cannot take off my cap."

But the Lady Guinevere, who stood beside the chair of King Leodegrance, spake and said: "I do beseech thee, Messire, for to take off thy cap unto my father."

Whereupon the gardener's boy said: "At thy bidding I will take it off."

So he took the cap from off his head, and King Leodegrance beheld his face and knew him. And when he saw who it was who stood before him, he made a great outcry from pure amazement. And he said: "My Lord and my King! What is this!" Thereupon he arose from where he sat, and he went and kneeled down upon the ground before King Arthur. And he set the palms of his hands together and he put his hands within the hands of King Arthur, and King Arthur took the hands of King Leodegrance within his own. And King Leodegrance said: "My Lord! My Lord! Is it then thou who hast done all these wonderful things?"

Then King Arthur said: "Yea; such as those things were, I have done them." And he stooped and kissed King Leodegrance upon the cheek and lifted him up unto his feet and gave him words of good cheer.

Now the Lady Guinevere, when she beheld those things that passed, was astonished beyond measure. And lo! she understood of a sudden all these things with amazing clearness. Wherefore a great fear fell upon her so that she trembled exceedingly, and said unto herself: "What things have I said unto this great King, and how have I made a mock of him and a jest of him before all those who were about me!" And at the thought thereof, she set her hand upon her side for to still the extreme disturbance of her heart. So, whilst King Arthur and King Leodegrance gave to one another words of royal greeting and of compliment, she withdrew herself and went and stood over against the window nigh to the corner of the wall.

Then, by and by, King Arthur lifted up his eyes and beheld her where she stood afar off. So he went straightway unto her and he took her by the hand, and he said: "Lady, what cheer?"

And she said: "Lord, I am afeard of thy greatness." And he said: "Nay, Lady. Rather it is I who am afeard of thee. For thy kind regard is dearer unto me than anything else in all the world, else had I not served for these twelve days as gardener's boy in thy garden all for the sake of thy good will." And she said: "Thou hast my good will, Lord." And he said: "Have I thy good will in great measure?" And she said: "Yea, thou hast it in great measure."

Then he stooped his head and kissed her before all those who were there, and thus their troth was plighted.

troth was plighted: Their promise of marriage was made.

Then King Leodegrance was filled with such an exceeding joy that he wist not how to contain himself therefore.

Now, after these things, there followed a war with King Ryence of North Wales. For Sir Kay and Sir Ulfius had gathered together a great army as King Arthur had bidden them to do, so that when King Ryence came against Cameliard he was altogether routed, and his army dispersed, and he himself chased, an outcast, into his mountains.

routed: Overthrown, defeated.

Then there was great rejoicing in Cameliard. For, after his victory, King Arthur remained there for awhile with an exceedingly splendid Court of noble lords and of beautiful ladies. And there was feasting and jousting and many famous bouts at arms, the like of which those parts had never before beheld. And King Arthur and the Lady Guinevere were altogether happy together.

Now, one day, whiles King Arthur sat at feast with King Leodegrance—they two being exceedingly expanded with cheerfulness—King Leodegrance said unto King Arthur: "My Lord, what shall I offer thee for a dowery with my daughter when thou takest her away from me for to be thy Queen?"

Then King Arthur turned to Merlin, who stood nigh to him, and he said: "Ha, Merlin! What shall I demand of my friend by way of that dowery?"

Unto him Merlin said: "My lord King, thy friend King Leodegrance hath one thing, the which, should he bestow it upon thee, will singularly increase the glory and renown of thy reign, so that the fame thereof shall never be forgotten."

And King Arthur said: "I bid thee, Merlin, tell me what is that thing."

So Merlin said: "My lord King, I will tell thee a story:

"In the days of thy father, Uther-Pendragon, I caused to be made for him a certain table in the shape of a ring, wherefore men called it the ROUND TABLE. Now, at this table were seats for fifty men, and these seats were designed for the fifty knights who were the most worthy knights in all the world. These seats were of such a sort, that whenever a worthy knight appeared, then his name appeared in letters of gold upon that seat that appertained unto him; and when that knight died, then would his name suddenly vanish from that seat which he had aforetime occupied.

"Now, forty-and-nine of these seats, except one seat, were altogether alike (saving only one that was set aside for the King himself, which same was elevated above the other seats, and was cunningly carved and inlaid with ivory and with gold), and the one seat was different from all the others, and it was called the SEAT PERILOUS. For this seat was unlike the others both in its structure and its significance; for it was **of curious device: Of skillful design.** all cunningly inset with gold and silver of curious device, and it was covered with a canopy of satin embroidered with gold and silver; and it was altogether of a wonderful magnificence of appearance. And no name ever appeared upon this seat, for only one knight in all of the world could hope to sit therein with safety unto himself. For, if any other dared to sit therein, either he would die a sudden and violent death within three days' time, or else a great misfortune would befall him. Hence that seat was called the SEAT PERILOUS.

"Now, in the days of King Uther-Pendragon, there sat seven-and-thirty knights at the ROUND TABLE. And when

King Uther-Pendragon died, he gave the ROUND TABLE unto his friend, King Leodegrance of Cameliard.

"And in the beginning of King Leodegrance's reign, there sat four-and-twenty knights at the ROUND TABLE.

"But times have changed since then, and the glory of King Leodegrance's reign hath paled before the glory of thy reign, so that his noble Court of knights have altogether quitted him. Wherefore there remaineth now not one name, saving only the name of King Leodegrance, upon all those fifty seats that surround the ROUND TABLE. So now that ROUND TABLE lieth beneath its pavilion altogether unused.

"Yet if King Leodegrance will give unto thee, my lord King, that ROUND TABLE for a dower with the Lady Guinevere, then will it lend unto thy reign its greatest glory. For in thy day every seat of that TABLE shall be filled, even unto the SEAT PERILOUS, and the fame of the knights who sit at it shall never be forgotten."

dower: Dowry, the wedding gift given by the bride's father to the groom.

"Ha!" quoth King Arthur. "That would indeed be a dower worthy for any king to have with his queen."

"Then," King Leodegrance said, "that dower shalt thou have with my daughter; and if it bring thee great glory, then shall thy glory be my glory, and thy renown shall be my renown. For if my glory shall wane, and thy glory shall increase, behold! is not my child thy wife?"

wane: Decline, decrease.

And King Arthur said: "Thou sayest well and wisely."

Thus King Arthur became the master of that famous ROUND TABLE. And the ROUND TABLE was set up at Camelot (which some men now call Winchester). And by and by there gathered about it such an array of knights as the world had never beheld before that time, and which it shall never behold again.

Such was the history of the beginning of the ROUND TABLE in King Arthur's reign.

And now was come the early fall of the year; that pleasant season when the meadow-land and the wold were still green with summer that had only just passed; when the sky likewise was as of summer-time—extraordinarily blue and full of large floating clouds; when a bird might sing here and another there, a short song in memory of spring-time, when all the air was tempered with warmth and yet the leaves were everywhere turning brown and red and gold, so that when the sun shone through them it was as though a cloth of gold, broidered with brown and crimson and green, hung above the head. At this season of the year it is exceedingly pleasant to be a-field among the nut-trees with hawk and hound, or to travel abroad in the yellow world, whether it be a-horse or a-foot.

Now this was the time of year in which had been set the marriage of King Arthur and the Lady Guinevere at Camelot, and at that place was extraordinary pomp and glory of circumstance. All the world was astir and in a great ferment of joy, for everybody was exceedingly glad that King Arthur was to have him a Queen.

6

HOW KING ARTHUR WAS WEDDED IN ROYAL STATE AND HOW THE ROUND TABLE WAS ESTABLISHED.

a-field with hawk and hound: To hunt with a hawk for catching birds and with a hound for tracking deer.
wold: Forest land.

175

In preparation for that great occasion the town of Camelot was bedight very magnificently, for the stony street along which the Lady Guinevere must come to the royal castle of the King was strewn thick with fresh-cut rushes smoothly laid. Moreover it was in many places spread with carpets of excellent pattern such as might be fit to lay upon the floor of some goodly hall. Likewise all the houses along the way were hung with fine hangings of woven texture interwoven with threads of azure and crimson, and everywhere were flags and banners afloat in the warm and gentle breeze against the blue sky, wherefore that all the world appeared to be alive with bright colors, so that when one looked adown that street, it was as though one beheld a crooked path of exceeding beauty and gayety stretched before him.

Thus came the wedding-day of the King—bright and clear and exceedingly radiant.

King Arthur sat in his hall surrounded by his Court awaiting news that the Lady Guinevere was coming thitherward. And it was about the middle of the morning when there came a messenger in haste riding upon a milk-white steed. And the raiment of that messenger and the trappings of his horse were all of cloth of gold embroidered with scarlet and white, and the tabard of the messenger was set with many jewels of various sorts so that he glistened from afar as he rode, with a singular splendor of appearance.

So this herald-messenger came straight into the castle where the King abided waiting, and he said: "Arise, my lord King, for the Lady Guinevere and her Court draweth nigh unto this place."

Upon this the King immediately arose with great joy, and straightway he went forth with his Court of Knights, riding in great state. And as he went down that marvellously adorned street, all the people shouted aloud as he passed by, wherefore he smiled and bent his head from side to side; for that day he was passing happy and loved his people with wonderful friendliness.

hangings: Tapestries.

Thus he rode forward unto the town gate, and out therefrom, and so came thence into the country beyond where the broad and well-beaten highway ran winding down beside the shining river betwixt the willows and the osiers.

And, behold! King Arthur and those with him perceived the Court of the Princess where it appeared at a distance, wherefore they made great rejoicing and hastened forward with all speed. And as they came nigh, the sun falling upon the apparels of silk and cloth of gold, and upon golden chains and the jewels that hung therefrom, all of that noble company that surrounded the Lady Guinevere and her litter flashed and sparkled with surpassing radiance.

For seventeen of the noblest knights of the King's Court, clad in complete armor, and sent by him as an escort unto the lady, rode in great splendor, surrounding the litter wherein the Princess lay. And the framework of that litter was of richly gilded wood, and its curtains and its cushions were of crimson silk embroidered with threads of gold. And behind the litter there rode in gay and joyous array, all shining with many colors, the Court of the Princess—her damsels in waiting, gentlemen, ladies, pages, and attendants.

So those parties of the King and the Lady Guinevere drew nigh together until they met and mingled the one with the other.

Then straightway King Arthur dismounted from his noble horse and, all clothed with royalty, he went afoot unto the Lady Guinevere's litter, whiles Sir Gawaine and Sir Ewaine held the bridle of his horse. Thereupon one of her pages drew aside the silken curtains of the Lady Guinevere's litter, and King Leodegrance gave her his hand and she straightway descended therefrom, all embalmed, as it were, in exceeding beauty. So King Leodegrance led her to King Arthur, and King Arthur came to her and placed one hand beneath her chin and the other upon her head and inclined his countenance and kissed her upon her smooth cheek—all warm and fragrant like velvet for softness, and without any blemish

THE WINNING OF A QUEEN

osiers: A kind of willow tree.

litter: A portable couch suspended between shafts and carried by men or horses.

177

whatsoever. And when he had thus kissed her upon the cheek, all those who were there lifted up their voices in great acclaim, giving loud voice of joy that those two noble souls had thus met together.

Thus did King Arthur give welcome unto the Lady Guinevere and unto King Leodegrance her father upon the highway beneath the walls of the town of Camelot, at the distance of half a league from that place. And no one who was there ever forgot that meeting, for it was full of extraordinary grace and noble courtliness.

Then King Arthur and his Court of Knights and nobles brought King Leodegrance and the Lady Guinevere with great ceremony unto Camelot and unto the royal castle, where apartments were assigned to all, so that the entire place was alive with joyousness and beauty.

And when high noon had come, the entire Court went with great state and ceremony unto the cathedral, and there, surrounded with wonderful magnificence, those two noble souls were married by the Archbishop.

And all the bells rang right joyfully, and all the people who stood without the cathedral shouted with loud acclaim, and lo! the King and the Queen came forth all shining, like unto the sun for splendor and like unto the moon for beauty.

In the castle a great noontide feast was spread, and there sat thereat four hundred, eighty and six lordly and noble folk—kings, knights, and nobles—with queens and ladies in magnificent array. And near to the King and the Queen there sat King Leodegrance and Merlin, and Sir Ulfius, and Sir Ector the trustworthy, and Sir Gawaine, and Sir Ewaine, and Sir Kay, and King Ban, and King Pellinore and many other famous and exalted folk, so that no man had ever beheld such magnificent courtliness as he beheld at that famous wedding-feast of King Arthur and Queen Guinevere.

And that day was likewise very famous in the history of

chivalry, for in the afternoon the famous Round Table was established, and that Round Table was at once the very flower and the chiefest glory of King Arthur's reign.

For about mid of the afternoon the King and Queen, preceded by Merlin and followed by all that splendid Court of kings, lords, nobles and knights in full array, made progression to that place where Merlin, partly by magic and partly by skill, had caused to be builded a very wonderful pavilion above the Round Table where it stood.

And when the King and the Queen and the Court had entered in thereat they were amazed at the beauty of that pavilion, for they perceived, an it were, a great space that appeared to be a marvellous land of Fay. For the walls were all richly gilded and were painted with very wonderful figures of saints and of angels, clad in ultramarine and crimson, and all those saints and angels were depicted playing upon various musical instruments that appeared to be made of gold. And overhead the roof of the pavilion was made to represent the sky, being all of cerulean blue sprinkled over with stars. And in the midst of that painted sky was an image, an it were, of the sun in his glory. And under foot was a pavement all of marble stone, set in squares of black and white, and blue and red, and sundry other colors.

In the midst of the pavilion was a Round Table with seats thereat exactly sufficient for fifty persons, and at each of the fifty places was a chalice of gold filled with fragrant wine, and at each place was a paten of gold bearing a manchet of fair white bread. And when the King and his Court entered into the pavilion, lo! music began of a sudden for to play with a wonderful sweetness.

Then Merlin came and took King Arthur by the hand and led him away from Queen Guinevere. And he said unto the King, "Lo! this is the Round Table."

Then King Arthur said, "Merlin, that which I see is wonderful beyond the telling."

depicted: Represented.

cerulean blue: Deep blue.

paten: A thin plate.

After that Merlin discovered unto the King the various marvels of the Round Table, for first he pointed to a high seat, very wonderfully wrought in precious woods and gilded so that it was exceedingly beautiful, and he said, "Behold, lord King, yonder seat is hight the 'Seat Royal,' and that seat is thine for to sit in." And as Merlin spake, lo! there suddenly appeared sundry letters of gold upon the back of that seat, and the letters of gold read the name,

Arthur, King.

And Merlin said, "Lord, yonder seat may well be called the centre seat of the Round Table, for, in sooth, thou art indeed the very centre of all that is most worthy of true knightliness. Wherefore that seat shall be called the centre seat of all the other seats."

Then Merlin pointed to the seat that stood opposite to the Seat Royal, and that seat also was of a very wonderful appearance as afore told in this history. And Merlin said unto the King: "My lord King, that seat is called the Seat Perilous, for no man but one in all this world shall sit therein, and that man is not yet born upon the earth. And if any other man shall dare to sit therein that man shall either suffer death or a sudden and terrible misfortune for his temerity. Wherefore that seat is called the Seat Perilous."

temerity: Boldness.

"Merlin," quoth the King, "all that thou tellest me passeth the bound of understanding for marvellousness. Now I do beseech thee in all haste for to find forthwith a sufficient number of knights to fill this Round Table so that my glory shall be entirely complete."

Then Merlin smiled upon the King, though not with cheerfulness, and said, "Lord, why art thou in such haste? Know that when this Round Table shall be entirely filled in all its seats, then shall thy glory be entirely achieved and then forthwith shall thy day begin for to decline. For when any

180

man hath reached the crowning of his glory, then his work is done and God breaketh him as a man might break a chalice from which such perfect ichor hath been drunk that no baser wine may be allowed to defile it. So when thy work is done and ended shall God shatter the chalice of thy life."

Then did the King look very steadfastly into Merlin's face, and said, "Old man, that which thou sayest is ever of great wonder, for thou speakest words of wisdom. Ne'theless, seeing that I am in God His hands, I do wish for my glory and for His good will to be accomplished even though He shall then entirely break me when I have served His purposes."

"Lord," said Merlin, "thou speakest like a worthy king and with a very large and noble heart. Ne'theless, I may not fill the Round Table for thee at this time. For, though thou hast gathered about thee the very noblest Court of Chivalry in all of Christendom, yet are there but two and thirty knights here present who may be considered worthy to sit at the Round Table."

"Then, Merlin," quoth King Arthur, "I do desire of thee that thou shalt straightway choose me those two and thirty."

"So will I do, lord King," said Merlin.

Then Merlin cast his eyes around and lo! he saw where King Pellinore stood at a little distance. Unto him went Merlin and took him by the hand. "Behold, my lord King," quoth he. "Here is the knight in all the world next to thyself who at this time is most worthy for to sit at this Round Table. For he is both exceedingly gentle of demeanor unto the poor and needy and at the same time is so terribly strong and skilful that I know not whether thou or he is the more to be feared in an encounter of knight against knight."

Then Merlin led King Pellinore forward and behold! upon the high seat that stood upon the left hand of the Royal Seat there appeared of a sudden the name,

𝕻ellinore.

ichor: Liquid. In Ancient Greece, it was believed that ichor, an ethereal fluid, ran in the veins of the Gods instead of blood.
chalice: A drinking cup or goblet.

And the name was emblazoned in letters of gold that shone with extraordinary lustre. And when King Pellinore took his seat, great and loud acclaim long continued was given him by all those who stood round about.

Then after that Merlin had thus chosen King Arthur and King Pellinore he chose out of the Court of King Arthur the following knights, two and thirty in all, and these were the knights of great renown in chivalry who did first establish the Round Table. Wherefore they were surnamed "The Ancient and Honorable Companions of the Round Table."

To begin, there was Sir Gawaine and Sir Ewaine, who were nephews unto the King, and they sat nigh to him upon the right hand; there was Sir Ulfius (who held his seat but four years and eight months unto the time of his death, after which Sir Geheris—who was esquire unto his brother, Sir Gawaine—held that seat); and there was Sir Kay the Seneschal, who was foster brother unto the King; and there was Sir Baudwain of Britain (who held his seat but three years and two months until his death, after the which Sir Agravaine held that seat); and there was Sir Pellias and Sir Geraint and Sir Constantine, son of Sir Caderes the Seneschal of Cornwall (which same was king after King Arthur); and there was Sir Caradoc and Sir Sagramore, surnamed the Desirous, and Sir Dinadan and Sir Dodinas, surnamed the Savage, and Sir Bruin, surnamed the Black, and Sir Meliot of Logres, and Sir Aglaval and Sir Durnure, and Sir Lamorac (which three young knights were sons of King Pellinore), and there was Sir Griflet and Sir Ladinas and Sir Brandiles and Sir Persavant of Ironside, and Sir Dinas of Cornwall, and Sir Brian of Listinoise, and Sir Palomides and Sir Degraine and Sir Epinogres, the son of the King of North Umberland and brother unto the enchantress Vivien, and Sir Lamiel of Cardiff, and Sir Lucan the Bottler and Sir Bedevere his brother (which same bare King Arthur unto the ship of Fairies when he lay so sorely wounded nigh unto death after the last battle which he fought). These two and thirty knights were the Ancient Companions of the Round Table, and unto them were added others until there were nine and forty in all, and then was added Sir Galahad, and with him the Round Table was made entirely complete.

Now as each of these knights was chosen by Merlin, lo! as he took that knight by the hand, the name of that knight suddenly appeared in golden letters, very bright and shining, upon the seat that appertained to him.

But when all had been chosen, behold! King Arthur saw that the seat upon the right hand of the Seat Royal had not been filled, and that it bare no name upon it. And he said unto Merlin: "Merlin, how is this, that the seat upon my right hand hath not been filled, and beareth no name?"

And Merlin said: "Lord, there shall be a name thereon in a very little while, and he who shall sit therein shall be the greatest knight in all the world until that the knight cometh who shall occupy the Seat Perilous. For he who cometh shall exceed all other men in beauty and in strength and in knightly grace."

And King Arthur said: "I would that he were with us now." And Merlin said: "He cometh anon."

Thus was the Round Table established with great pomp and great ceremony of estate. For first the Archbishop of Canterbury blessed each and every seat, progressing from place to place surrounded by his Holy Court, the choir whereof singing most musically in accord, whiles others swung censers from which there ascended an exceedingly fragrant vapor of frankincense, filling that entire pavilion with an odor of Heavenly blessedness.

Censer

And when the Archbishop had thus blessed every one of those seats, the chosen knight took each his stall at the Round Table, and his esquire came and stood behind him, holding the banneret with his coat-of-arms upon the spear-point above the knight's head. And all those who stood about that place, both knights and ladies, lifted up their voices in loud acclaim.

Then all the knights arose, and each knight held up before him the cross of the hilt of his sword, and each knight spake word for word as King Arthur spake. And this was the covenant of their Knighthood of the Round Table: That they would be gentle unto the weak; that they would be courageous unto the strong; that they would be terrible unto the wicked and the evil-doer; that they would defend the helpless who should call upon them for aid; that all women should be held unto them sacred; that they would stand unto the defence of one another whensoever such defence should be required; that they would be merciful unto all men; that they would be gentle of deed, true in friendship, and faithful in love. This was their covenant, and unto it each knight sware upon the cross of his sword, and in witness thereof did kiss the hilt thereof. Thereupon all who stood thereabouts once more gave loud acclaim.

Then all the knights of the Round Table seated themselves, and each knight brake bread from the golden patten, and quaffed wine from the golden chalice that stood before him, giving thanks unto God for that which he ate and drank.

Thus was King Arthur wedded unto Queen Guinevere, and thus was the Round Table established.

covenant: Mutual promise or vow.

Backword

HOWARD PYLE
THE MAN WHO MADE LEGENDS COME ALIVE

The war with Mexico was over; the Civil War had not begun. Gold from California was flowing into the eastern United States when Howard Pyle was born in 1853, in Wilmington, Delaware.

Howard was a tall, gangling boy, friendly in a quiet way. He certainly was not the most brilliant student at the Quaker school he attended. Arithmetic and grammar were a bore. He was more interested in drawing pictures on his slate or in the margins of his books.

If he had no great love for Wilmington schools, Howard had a secret school of his own that he did love, one in which he was the only student. This was the garden that fronted his home. Years later he wrote, "In front of the house was a grassy lawn with a terraced bank (I used to roll over and over down that bank in the soft, warm grass on a summer's day), and there was a little grove, or park, of trees to one side and beyond you could see the turnpike. I remember that every now and then there would be a train of Conestoga wagons. . .They looked like great clumsy ships that had come from afar, and sometimes the leading team of eight mules, bedecked with gay harness trimmed with crimson leather and brass, was adorned with silver bells that rang a merry tune as it passed along the highway. On the other side of the house, to a little distance, was a garden of old, old-fashioned roses and sweet shrubs that filled the air with fragrance when they bloomed."

First Pictures

Inside the house were scores of good books free for the reading as well as the best illustrated magazines of the day. "I can remember," Howard wrote, "many and many an hour in which I lay stretched out before the fire in the snug, warm little library, whilst the

hickory logs snapped and crackled in the fireplace." Tenniel, who illustrated *Alice in Wonderland,* was one of his favorites. His mother, who had dreamed of being an artist herself, praised Howard's first drawings. She introduced him to many books.

It was through her faith in Howard's talent that his parents decided to send him to a small art school, taught by a Mr. Van der Weilen. For three years Howard studied with a man who knew how to draw and knew how to teach. He received a solid foundation in the techniques of drawing.

When he was 23, working for his father who was a leather merchant, and drawing in his spare time, Howard happened to visit Chincoteague, an island off the coast of Virginia. It captured his imagination: the sand

and scrub beaches, the smart, tough, little wild ponies that roamed the island, the rugged inhabitants who caught them. He returned home glowing with the color and character of what he had seen. He then wrote and illustrated an article about the island of Chincoteague. Extraordinary was his artist's eye for sharp, interesting detail which he carried over into his writing. He seemed to paint word pictures through which readers could visualize all that he described.

When Howard had finished, his mother urged him to send the article to a publisher. He sent it to *Scribner's Monthly,* which promptly bought it and urged him to come to New York.

His Career Begins

Howard's first few years in New York were difficult. At first he did both writing and illustrating. The great children's magazine, *St. Nicholas,* used many of his illustrated fables, but the pay was very small. He decided he had better concentrate on illustrations. One important magazine, *Harper's Weekly,* accepted many of his sketches but had them redrawn by a staff artist. The printer needed a detailed line drawing before he could reproduce the picture, and the editor doubted Howard's skill.

Finally Howard got his chance. After six weeks in seclusion, working steadily on one drawing, he submitted to his editor a dramatic scene in a lighthouse which he called, "Wreck in the Offing!" "I realized that this might be the turning point in my life," he wrote. "I can recall just how the art editor looked at me over his spectacles. . . . When he said that they were not only going to use it, but were going to make of it a double-page cut, my exaltation was so great that it seemed to me that I knew not where I was standing or what had happened to me. As I went away, I walked upon air—I seemed to float. I found a friend and I took him to Delmonico's and we had a lunch of all the delicacies in season and out of season."

That picture *was* a turning point. When it was published, in 1878, the public and other artists liked it, and Howard began to get all the work he could do.

Robin Hood

The Merry Adventures of Robin Hood of Great Renown in Nottinghamshire was published in 1883. Howard Pyle wrote and illustrated it with great care and supervised every detail of the printing and binding. The book was a work of art. Artists and writers reviewed it enthusiastically. William Morris, the British poet, artist, and maker of fine books, who thought that nothing good artistically could come out of America, had to admit that this was a well-made book. It was not immedi-

ately popular with the reading public, perhaps because of its huge price, but as years went by, it became one of the "best sellers" for children.

With his career assured, Howard returned to Wilmington, married Anne Poole, and once more started to write. The boy who had shown such little interest in school now had a tremendous flair for accurate information. He had an amazing knowledge of American history. "That man," said one of his admirers, "can tell you in an instant the color of the hat General Wolfe wore at Quebec."

"Not only that," remarked another, "give him the name of any Revolutionary regiment, and he can tell you the number of buttons on the uniforms of the officers!"

Knights of the Round Table

Howard wrote many other stories and books for children. The King Arthur series is perhaps his greatest. It took him seven years to do the necessary research, writing, and illustrating. The legends of King Arthur were simply, straightforwardly retold in four volumes. Howard used homely, somewhat archaic language, with a touch of the poetic. He also wrote *Men of Iron,* set in the England of Henry IV, and *Otto of the Silver Hand,* set in Medieval Germany.

The Pyles and their children spent some time every summer in Rehoboth, a little seaside town on the Delaware coast. An old lighthouse stands outside the town and the surrounding sand dunes creep up to a gnarled pine forest. The townspeople still tell legends of pirate treasure buried in the dunes.

Pyle wrote and illustrated several stories about buccaneers and buried treasure. Blackbeard was one of his favorite characters. The best of these stories he later collected and published under the title, *Howard Pyle's Book of Pirates.*

In addition to the stories he wrote and illustrated, Pyle was one of the foremost magazine illustrators of his day. Mark Twain said he was the only artist to do the illustrations for *Joan of Arc.* Pyle illustrated Oliver Wendell Holmes' humorous poem, "One-Hoss-Shay." He illustrated Woodrow Wilson's biography of George Washington, which was published in *Harper's.* Walter Reed, in his book, *The Illustrator in America,* says, ". . . the illustrations of Howard Pyle. . . are as exciting now as they were sixty years ago, while pictures by many of his contemporaries today look dated and mannered. . . . Pyle was interested in pictures, first of all, as drama."

Pyle as Teacher

From 1894 to 1900, Pyle taught a class in illustration at the Drexel Institute in Philadelphia and later he lectured to the Art Students League in New York. He wanted to free his students from the cramping influence of academic theories about drawing. He said, "I set them to work before the draped model, telling them not to copy the model but to make a picture, and I explained what was the difference between creative and imitative art."

A summer class in the country at Chadds Ford enabled Pyle to give intensive training to a few specially talented pupils. He persuaded the Institute to give scholarships to a certain number of students and he donated his services. The best pictures of his students were sent on to art editors and some of his students began to make almost enough money to support themselves. "You will learn more in one week of actual work," he wrote to one student, "than you can learn in two months of school study."

Pyle had already been notably successful as both writer and illustrator. Now he wished to crown his career with mural painting. He went to Italy to study the work of the old masters in order to train himself for this new and demanding field of art. He flung himself into his studies with his characteristic ardor and energy. Fate decided against him, however, for he died while he was abroad.

His vigorous pictures have brought alive the color and flavor of times long past. His tales of romance, knighthood, and high adventure are equally vivid. When he describes dawn, one feels the freshness of early morning in the forest. His "men of iron," the knights of the age of chivalry, are "men of heart" as well, with human trials and rewards—as true today as then. He took the ancient Celtic cycle of Arthurian legend, among the great stories of the world, and retold it with a warmth and charm which have given continued delight to thousands of children.

KING
ARTHUR'S
ENGLAND

The Arthurian Legend

No one knows for sure whether there was really a King Arthur, though there may have been an Anglo-Saxon or Celtic knight named Arthur whose nobility and bravery inspired a minstrel to sing a story of his adventures. From some such beginning, more than a thousand years ago, the legend of King Arthur and the Knights of the Round Table has grown and has been told in many ways. The legend of Arthur serves as a model for other legends of the time in which the hero, like Arthur, is an ideal specimen of chivalric honor and courage.

In medieval England, lords and earls were entertained by singers and storytellers called *scops*. The scops very often used for their subject the deeds of knights, which they glorified in song. They exaggerated the truth, and added to it. They added so much to the Arthurian story-song that many knights in the story also developed legends of their own.

The Arthurian legend developed throughout the whole medieval period in England. The first written mention of Arthur comes from about the year 800. In the late fifteenth century, Sir Thomas Malory collected all the tales of King Arthur that he could find, and from them wrote the book *Morte Darthur*. When the printing press was brought to England, *Morte Darthur* was published in 1485. It was one of the first books to be published in England, and formed the basis for most stories of King Arthur to follow. Five centuries later, Alfred, Lord Tennyson based his series

of poems, *The Idylls of the King* on his reading of *Morte Darthur*. Today's musical play, *Camelot,* is a modern addition to the rich tradition of Arthurian legend. Why is the Arthurian legend still alive, and the basis for a modern musical play? The answer might well be that King Arthur was the bravest, noblest knight of all—real or imagined—and that knights were the bravest and noblest of men.

Feudalism in England

For several centuries prior to the year 1066, England was ruled by Anglo-Saxons. They invaded England from Germany at about the same time the Huns were invading Rome. By the end of the seventh century, the Romans had given up their interest in England and the Anglo-Saxons had assumed complete control.

There were many variations on the basic idea of feudalism, and the Anglo-Saxons implanted their own brand of feudalism in England. In their society, the warrior was the greatest hero. The warriors were the ruling class of the early Anglo-Saxon society, and all of the work—the farming, fishing, carpentry, stone masonry, metal smithing, and all other forms of labor—was done by slaves, the hostages from previous conquests. The warriors, who passed their rule from father to son, were called *earls,* while the slaves were called *churls.* Later, earls became known as lords and kings.

The earl and his family lived in a castle, while the churls lived outside it in crude wood and sod huts, and wore coarse cloth and animal skin clothing. The earls dressed in the finest cloth of the day.

Despite their bondage, and living conditions that would seem cruel to us today, the churls' life was not totally grim. They did no work on Sundays, and there were many religious holidays—so many, in fact, that the churls worked only about half of the year. And on working days, they worked only in the morning and evening rather than all day. During the middle of the day some worked at hobbies, and often gave their handicraft to their masters. For exceptional service to his lord, a churl, or *serf,* would be set free. He had no nobility, despite his freedom, but could go from castle to castle selling his wares, or simply enjoy an easier life within his former master's castle. He was then called a *freeman.*

The overlord of a castle was called a king, and there were many kings in England during the Anglo-Saxon period. They fought constantly with each other. They sometimes formed agreements among themselves in order to conquer mutual enemies. A king's knights would usually consist of his relatives and friends, and because theirs was a warrior society, they did not fight to protect a lady's honor. Women, in fact, were in the same category as serfs. They did domestic chores and were not thought of too highly.

Much of this changed, though, when William the Conqueror and the Norman French under his command invaded England in the year 1066. William became the absolute overlord of all England, and thus established greater order than the Anglo-Saxons had been able to. The social order changed. Women were revered, and knights dedicated themselves to their ladies, fought for them, and wrote poems for them. Women themselves began to hold important social positions. They became members of the king's court instead of servants to it. When women became objects of praise rather than objects of scorn, they passed their time walking in their gardens, playing musical instruments, and generally being entertained as they wished.

While the feudal system had many faults compared with today's democratic society, it did much to form the modern world. As freemen became numerous, they formed what is today called the middle class. Women, for

the first time, were thought of romantically. And the knights contributed a great deal to our ideas of heroes and heroism.

Religion and Superstition

Medieval England was a melting pot of Christianity and Pagan religions. Druidism, Norse mythology, and astrology comprised the main superstitions of the Celts, Anglo-Saxons, and Normans of medieval England. This folklore, along with the Christianity brought to England by missionaries of the Roman Church and the great Irish Saint, Saint Patrick, combined to produce the belief of the day.

The Celts of early England believed in *Druidism,* in which the oak tree symbolized supernatural powers. They burned human sacrifices, usually young women. The religion was very elaborate, and the traditional Yule Log and Christmas tree are results of the mingling of Druid customs with Christianity.

Astrology and the wheel of fortune mingled with Christianity in some interesting ways. The wheel of fortune resembled the Zodiac, and both implied that a man was to live his life according to a pre-set pattern, or fate. The Christian missionaries taught an opposite idea—that a man could choose between God and the Devil. Many Englishmen of the Middle Ages (most of whom could not read or write), feared God, and hoped that He had set a good pattern in the stars for them to follow.

The Anglo-Saxons, along with the Vikings, believed in the Norse god *Odin,* and in the heaven reserved for warriors and heroes, *Valhalla.* Later, many Christian knights believed that God would grant them special favor if they died in valor on the battlefield.

The Christian monks, in monastaries in England and Europe, preserved the only books that were not destroyed by the warring feudal lords during the Middle Ages. They were guardians of both knowledge and the faith, and were highly regarded by the kings as advisors. Thus, priests were on nearly the same social scale as the kings themselves.

The Knight and His Code

Perhaps the most important member of the medieval English culture, the one around whom the rest of the society revolved, was the knight. He had his beginnings in the Anglo-Saxon warrior days, and reached his fullest development during the Norman period. As an Anglo-Saxon, the knight was simply a soldier and a hero. After the Norman invasion of England, he became much more. He had a strong ethical code. He was loyal to his king, and loyal to his lady. When not engaged in battle, he roamed the countryside in search of adventure. During such times, he was called a *knight-errant.* He was the champion of the underdog—any serf who was being robbed or beaten had a friend in any knight that happened to be passing by. *The Story of King Arthur* tells of an Anglo-Saxon king, with the ideals of a Norman. It is easy to see, as the legend of Arthur grew and things were added along the way, how it came to contain a cross-section of Anglo-Saxon and Norman life.

The knight performed most of his brave deeds from horseback. His brave and gentle behavior thus became known as *chivalry,* from the French word *cheval,* for horse. The knight's code was his chivalric code, and his gallant deeds were called chivalrous.

For sport, and to impress their ladies, who could not watch them in real battle, the knights would have tournaments in which they simulated battle. These were called *Lists,* and *Courts of Chivalry.* The knights on their war horses, all clad in armor, would ride at each other and try to knock each other out of the saddle with spears. Very often the ends of the spears were padded to prevent serious injury.

The Lists must have been quite a spectacle: all the royalty, and each knight's favorite lady, would gather in bleachers to watch. All were dressed in their finest costumes. The serfs might even take some time off to watch the proceedings from a distance. There would be great pomp and pageantry as heralds would sound trumpets, announcements would be made, and the knights, each with the help of at least one second, would prepare for mock battle. Then they would ride at each other, spears, padded like big boxing gloves on sticks, in hand. The unlucky knights would be bumped off their horses and fall to the ground with a heavy crunch. As their armor outweighed them, they would lie helpless, kicking and flailing, until rescued by their seconds.

This would continue until only one knight remained seated on his horse. And this brave knight—champion of all in tournament, who would ride fearlessly into battle though hopelessly outnumbered, the bravest of the brave—would tremble while his lady bestowed an honor upon him for winning the tournament. And, perhaps, even a kiss. A priest might say a blessing, and the knight would thank God and his lucky stars; then they would all join in a great feast, with much laughter and merrymaking. Then the serfs, silently watching from a distance, would quietly return to work in their fields.

Arthur, the king and the man, was the embodiment of all the brave and heroic Celts who battled against the Saxon invaders. The wars were waged in vain, and Arthur, the leader of the Celtic tribes, became the victor only in the fields of imagination. And imagination enriched the legends and songs so that he becomes the most gallant, the most magnanimous—the perfect—warrior and knight. In spite of the mythological coloring of the adventurous stories of King Arthur, the legend is brought more vividly to life because he is *probably* part of the historical past.